Persistence of Memory

Persistence of Memory

Amelia Atwater-Rhodes

DELACORTE PRESS

Published by Delacorte Press
an imprint of Random House Children's Books
a division of Random House, Inc.
New York

Visit us on the Web! www.randomhouse.com/teens

Educators and librarians, for a variety of teaching tools, visit us at
www.randomhouse.com/teachers

Library of Congress Cataloging-in-Publication Data
Atwater-Rhodes, Amelia.
Persistence of memory / by Amelia Atwater-Rhodes. — 1st American ed.
p. cm.
Summary: Diagnosed with schizophrenia as a child, sixteen-year-old Erin has spent
half of her life in therapy, but now must face the possibility of weird things in the real
world, including shapeshifting friends and her "alter," a centuries-old vampire.
ISBN 978-0-385-73437-0 (trade hardcover)—ISBN 978-0-385-90443-8
(Gibraltar lib. bdg.)
[1. Supernatural—Fiction. 2. Schizophrenia—Fiction. 3. Mental illness—Fiction.
4. Vampires—Fiction. 5. Witches—Fiction.] I. Title.
PZ7.A8925Per 2008
[Fic]—dc22
2008016062

The text of this book is set in 12-point Requiem.
Book design by Trish Parcell
Printed in the United States of America

10 9 8 7 6 5 4 3

First Edition

Persistence of Memory *is dedicated to Jesse, Dale, Nathan, and Angel, best of friends and family; and to Bri, Zim, Ria, and Mason for their tireless support, as readers, as fellow writers, and most importantly as dear friends.*

I would also like to give thanks to:

. . . my mother, who deserves more gratitude than I could possibly express for her unconditional love and willingness to encourage all my dreams. For this book, I also owe her many thanks for her expert knowledge about Massachusetts public school policy and procedures.

. . . Mandi, for knowing when I need to be dragged away from the computer no matter how much work I need to do. You're amazing, darling.

. . . Tineke, for helping me through hard times. I really do listen to you, even if it sometimes takes me a long time to follow your advice.

. . . Professor Carol Smith at UMB, whose Psych 101 class and initial advising changed my life. Thank you also to Professor Adams, Professor Wainwright, and Professor Perez in the psychology department; and to Professor Wilfredo Chiesa in the art department, without whom I never would have imagined I could draw or paint.

. . . the CCHS Women's Fencing Team, and all the amazing individuals who so inspired me there.

. . . North Five, for taking such good care of people I love—and hello to the gentleman who works there who is a fan of mine.

. . . NaNoWriMo, and everyone who pushed me to sign up in 2006, which helped me finally find my spark of inspiration again.

. . . Jodi, who always pushes me to make a story the best it can be.

And, as always, to the exuberant support of the chat room and the message board. Without you, I never would have had the drive and courage to finish this story. Thank you for chocolate soy milk and saganaki.

A DREAM WITHIN A DREAM

Take this kiss upon the brow!
And, in parting from you now,
Thus much let me avow—
You are not wrong, who deem
That my days have been a dream;
Yet if hope has flown away
In a night, or in a day,
In a vision, or in none,
Is it therefore the less gone?
All that we see or seem
Is but a dream within a dream.

I stand amid the roar
Of a surf-tormented shore,
And I hold within my hand
Grains of the golden sand—
How few! yet how they creep
Through my fingers to the deep,
While I weep—while I weep!
O God! can I not grasp
Them with a tighter clasp?
O God! can I not save
One from the pitiless wave?
Is all that we see or seem
But a dream within a dream?

EDGAR ALLAN POE

Prologue

THE ALMOST-FULL OCTOBER MOON cast silver streaks across le Canal du Midi. To the east and west, bustling shops and hotels brightened the French cities of Sète and Toulouse even at this late hour, but here the water flowed, watched only by the hunter's moon above and the huntress below.

Shevaun walked silently along the canal, her bare feet immune to damp and chill. Her posture and expression were nonchalant, but she was aware of everything around her, most specifically the five men stalking her.

She had noticed one of the hunters following her back in Sète, but he had been wise enough not to accost her in front of other people. As soon as she had left the crowds, she had become aware of two more hunters, stinking of adrenaline and the oil they used to clean their blades.

Two more hunters were waiting by one of the canal's

bridges, just a hundred yards or so farther on. That was surely where they intended to ambush her.

One, dressed in the gaudy clothes of a tourist, a bottle of wine and a camera near at hand, lay on the bank just before the bridge.

Shevaun sniffed with disdain. She had lived through the fall of the Byzantine Empire. Now, five hundred years later, they expected to trap her like *this*?

Shevaun ignored the bait and went straight for the hook: the hunter concealed beneath the bridge. He let out a yelp as she wrapped her pale fingers around his throat, baring her fangs as she wrenched a knife from his hand. The "bait" sprang to his feet with a cry and darted to his companion's aid; the three hunters who had been following her gave up their stealth and raced toward the fight.

At last. Shevaun had been waiting *days* for this group to stop hiding and make its move. Five against one was, at least, a fight worth having.

Chapter 1

IT WASN'T SUPPOSED TO BE physically possible for Erin to be awake at one in the morning. The medication she had taken after dinner—a handful of pills in a multitude of shapes and colors—should have put her to sleep a long time ago. Normally they did.

But tonight she was still wide awake.

She crossed to the window and looked out at the October sky. A few wispy clouds failed to hide the stars and a brilliant moon a few days from full. Erin pushed open the window and breathed in the chilly air.

She could do that. It was her window. It wasn't locked. It wasn't shatter-proof. She was grateful. *Grateful,* damn it.

Erin sat on the floor beneath the window, tears suddenly in her eyes. This was *stupid.* Why wasn't she asleep?

Her stomach growled, giving her a good excuse to push

herself to her feet and pad across her carpeted floor to her bedroom door. She crept downstairs and snagged an apple from the fridge, but she felt queasy after two bites.

Go to bed, Erin, she told herself. *You have to be up for school in a couple of hours.*

She didn't know why she felt so restless, but the anxiety was like a constant itch. None of the dozens of relaxation and focusing exercises she had been taught by perhaps a hundred doctors during her sixteen years of life seemed able to calm it.

Halfway back up the stairs, she heard her father's voice. "Erin? Is that you?"

"It's me," she called back.

"Something wrong?"

"Just went to get a snack. I'm going back to bed."

He gave her a worried look as she passed him in the hallway. After all, it was one in the morning, and she was swaying as she walked, bumping into things and apparently making enough of a ruckus to wake him and make him fear that his worst nightmares could be coming true. The window was hers to open . . . as was the front door. If she had been quieter—and in a different mind-set—she could have walked out, and it would have been hours before her father even noticed.

She crossed her arms on her chest and shivered. If she had walked out, it could have been hours before even *she* noticed.

"Sleep well," her father said, unaware of her thoughts. "Remember you have to be up at six."

"Ugh. Don't remind me."

There was a photo album on the bookshelf in her room, and Erin picked it up on her way to bed. The cover was fabric, embroidered with the image of a phoenix aflame. The pages inside were laminated.

She didn't look through the pictures right then, just lay down, wrapped her arms around the album, and tugged the blankets over herself.

Too soon, it was morning and she was sitting in her English class, stifling a yawn and doodling. The fact of the matter was, Juliet was an idiot and Romeo was even dumber. Erin didn't *care* if it was a tragedy or a comedy; she didn't care what great scholars thought about the play. Frankly, the "greatest" love story ever written didn't appeal to her a whole lot. Who killed herself over someone she had just met four days earlier?

Even Erin wasn't *that* crazy.

Oh, wait, not "crazy." That word wasn't politically correct, according to the school counselor Erin had been forced to speak to before she was allowed to attend afternoon classes at their shiny public institution. Erin saw some of the best psychologists and psychiatrists in the nation on a daily basis. Even the woman droning on about the lewd humor in *Romeo and Juliet* was a nurse and a licensed clinical psychologist in addition to being an English teacher qualified to instruct students with moderate to severe psychiatric disabilities.

They all knew that her using the blanket term "crazy" wasn't the heart of her problems.

"Erin?" Her teacher prompted her.

"Huh?" she said with a guilty start, instinctively slapping a hand down over her drawing. "I'm sorry," she added. "I didn't sleep well. I spaced."

Unfortunately, pretending she had been listening wasn't really an option in a class with only two other students, especially given the fairly detailed sketch of—

Aww, crap.

Her teacher glanced at the drawing before Erin could subtly turn to a fresh page. The sketch had been done swiftly, but Erin's drawing skills had betrayed her, making its contents very clear: it was the sword fight in which Romeo killed Tybalt—specifically, the exact moment when he stabbed him.

"I—no," Erin protested before her teacher could say a single word. "It's nothing. A girl in my afternoon classes is trying to convince me to join the fencing team, so I was thinking about . . ." Stabbing people? "It's a scene from the play, anyway, not . . . It's just a *doodle!*" Erin sighed. She had lost the argument without her instructor-psychologist needing to say a word. Erin put down her pen, defeated. "Can I just go see Tina *now*? If I wait until after class, I'll miss the midterm review for AP Chemistry."

Her teacher nodded, and Erin left the classroom and crossed to Dr. Tina Vaughan's office. She and Tina had worked together for two years, since Erin had left full-time hospitals and started taking classes at this outpatient private school. Erin *mostly* trusted her not to overreact.

She knocked and then stepped into Tina's office. She handed over the drawing with a frustrated "hmph" as she sank into a quite familiar overstuffed armchair.

"Are these your English notes?" Tina asked, her voice neutral.

Erin shrugged. It was stupid, but she hadn't been paying attention to what she was drawing on the page. She rarely did; if she had a pen or a pencil in her hand, she was always drawing. Well, except that one time she had stabbed a nurse in the hand, but that had been a *long* time ago.

Three years ago, at least.

"I was thinking about fencing and the scene in the book and it just came out," Erin said. "It doesn't mean anything. If I were thinking of stabbing someone, why would I have *drawn* it?" That line of argument wasn't going to help. "I'm sorry. I didn't sleep well, and I'm all nervous about my chemistry exam, and I just don't *care* about *Romeo and Juliet.*" In a forced attempt at humor, she added, "Sometimes a cigar is just a cigar, right?"

"Sometimes," Tina said as she passed back the drawing. "You understand why we have to respond to something like this, though, right?"

Erin sighed. "Yeah. 'History of violent behavior.' Bad mix with drawings of people being stabbed."

Tina nodded. "Is there anything we need to talk about?"

"It was just a response to the book," Erin said. "Nothing more."

Even so, Erin knew she wasn't about to get off the hook quite so easily. She had been symptom-free for eighteen months, long enough that her therapist trusted her to an extent, but that didn't mean there wouldn't be a little prying just in case.

"You're still having trouble in your chemistry class?"

"It's AP," Erin said defensively. "And I'm not used to such a large class. It's a different kind of learning."

Languages had always come easily to her. She was already fluent in Italian, French, and Latin and spoke some Greek and a little Spanish. She read and comprehended literature at the college level when she bothered to pay attention; she had a knack for remembering historical facts and dates; and she hadn't had any trouble with biology or her math courses.

But AP Chemistry, taught in a classroom of thirty-two people at a neighboring public high school, was the first subject she had ever studied that was a struggle. She didn't like it.

"It's good you're being challenged," Tina insisted. "That was one reason we wanted to transition you into the public school this year. You've advanced beyond what we can offer you here."

Erin smirked. "And here I thought it was just because the public school was sick of paying for private education."

Every child in Massachusetts was legally entitled to a

"free and public education," and if the public school couldn't safely provide that for a student, it had to pay for the student's placement in an institution that could. Erin had been out of the public school system since second grade. If everything went well that semester at Nefershen Public High School, she would have a full course schedule the next year and see her shrink only once a week.

Erin still didn't think this was a good idea, but that hadn't swayed the board of education; or her plethora of psychologists, psychiatrists, and teachers; or her father. None of them seemed to remember that she *wasn't* a normal girl, and if things *didn't* go well, that meant she might have . . .

"Regardless, it *is* good for you to be dealing with some harder subjects. Are you still helping tutor that girl from your French class?"

"Yeah," Erin answered, shifting nervously. "Marissa's actually in my chem class, too, so she's been helping me there. But I *really* don't want to miss the exam review."

Tina glanced at the clock. "You've got time."

Erin leaned back again in the chair and added, "Marissa is the captain of the fencing team. Their season starts today, and she's been pushing me to join. It's hard to tell her that I can't."

"You didn't mention you were thinking of joining a sports team," Tina said, surprised.

"I'm not *thinking* of it," Erin responded quickly. "I'm not even supposed to *draw* a sword fight. I don't think you guys would love the idea of my participating in one. It's just that . . ." She hesitated, trying to be careful with what she said so that she wouldn't raise any more red flags that day. "It's nice to have a friend at school, and I don't want to let her down. And I like the idea of being invited to do things the other kids do."

"Are you just worried about what *I* will say if you join the team," Tina asked, "or are you having troubling thoughts on the matter?"

"I'm not worried I'm going to hurt anyone. Marissa says they're all really well protected, and the equipment's blunt. The way she described it made fencing seem . . ." She stopped to search for the right word. ". . . civilized. A lot of the rules date back to old-fashioned notions of chivalry. It sounds nice."

Tina was smiling and nodding. "See? Most sports activities out of context would be considered abnormal. It isn't considered healthy to throw things at people, but baseball is the national pastime. You're at a point where you can separate healthy competition from aggression in your mind, and where you can recognize the difference between disciplined, rule-based sports and *violence.* I think it would be good for you to get involved in some kind of sport. If nothing else, it would be nice for you to get your exercise in a more social manner than you can in our gym."

Erin bit her lip. She had thought—hoped, if she was honest—that Tina would discourage her or even outright forbid her to participate in such an activity. Now if Erin said no, she would have to live with the knowledge that it was out of cowardice.

"I'm not sure I'm ready for that kind of social activity," she admitted quietly.

Tina squeezed Erin's hand supportively. "You were nervous about transitioning back to public school, too, but you seem to be happy with how that's going. I won't force you into any kind of extracurricular activity, but I'm certainly not going to forbid it, either. It's up to you."

Erin cringed. The world was safer when fewer things were left up to her.

Chapter 2

"WOULD YOU FREAK OUT if I tried to join a sports team?"
Erin asked her father as he signed her out of her morning
classes.

"I would be happy to see you doing something you
enjoy," he answered carefully, "and having fun with kids at
school. I was on the football team when I was your age,
and it was probably the best part of my high school days."

Erin tried to resist the impulse to frown. Why couldn't
he have joined the chess team, or even run cross-country?
Something *less* dangerous than fencing?

"You never mentioned that you were a jock," she said,
trying to make it a joke since he sounded so serious.

He shrugged. "Never came up."

She knew that really meant "I didn't bring it up because
I didn't know if you would ever be able to do the same."

Okay, then. She would try.

It couldn't hurt to try, right?

*　*　*

Erin and Marissa were assigned seats on opposite sides of their French classroom, and Erin was too busy marking up notes during chemistry even to think about talking to Marissa. At the end of the school day, Erin walked with her to their usual spot outside at the edge of the sports fields, where they sat on a short stone wall with their notebooks balanced on their knees.

Two inches shorter than Erin, Marissa was a petite Asian girl who always wore jeans and a T-shirt, regardless of the temperature, and yet she somehow had an undeniably intimidating presence, especially whenever one of "her" fencers walked by. She tended to address her teammates in loud, rapid sentences and then drop abruptly back into the subdued, embarrassed manner in which she responded to her French assignments.

"Somehow you have trouble getting people to join the team, with a pitch like that?" Erin asked after one of these tirades.

"Eh, Karen will stick around," Marissa said. "Trust me. Athletic types feel the need for a firm, controlling hand."

"Uh-huh," Erin said, though she had thought the same thing about herself just a few hours before. "Let's look at your essay, shall we?"

Marissa gave her an odd look, and Erin shrugged. "Reading too much Shakespeare," she said. "Next I'll be using words like 'thou' and 'wherefore' casually. Your essay?"

"I don't think I really . . ." Marissa withered beneath

Erin's patiently firm gaze, which she had learned from many excellent therapists. "I mean, I should . . . Oh, *here*!"

She handed over the paper, and Erin quickly discovered why she had been hesitant. "Did you use an online translator to write this?"

Marissa blushed. "I was in a hurry."

"Well, you're implying you're doing obscene things with a cow here," Erin said, circling a passage, "so you might want to consider editing a little before you turn it in."

Marissa laughed. "How did you learn all this, anyway? You said you were homeschooled or something, right?"

Erin hesitated. Early in the semester, she had said something vague about why she didn't have morning classes. Marissa had misinterpreted, and Erin hadn't bothered to correct her. Now, though, she felt bad lying to someone who had become a friend.

"Private schooled," she said, "for medical reasons. I don't really want to talk about it."

"Sure," Marissa agreed reluctantly, obviously still curious. "Look, this essay is crap not even worth your time. Let's go over electron configurations again before we have to go to practice."

"Before *you* have to go to practice," Erin corrected her absently.

"I asked the coach," Marissa said. "She says that you have a right to be on the team as long as you're attending classes here, no matter what the rest of your situation is."

"Maybe I'll . . ." Erin bit her lip as she saw Marissa's face light up. "Can I just *watch* practice, for a day? To get a sense of what it's like?"

Marissa deflated just a little but seemed to accept that this was as close to an agreement as she was going to get for the moment. "Sure. I'll tell the coach not to harass you."

I should be studying, Erin thought as she followed Marissa to the gym. That would have been a perfectly reasonable excuse for getting out of joining the team.

It was too late, though. Marissa was introducing Erin to the team's coach and explaining that Erin would be watching practice. Coach McCallan gave her a stern look and said that though she was welcome to watch, under no circumstances was she to go anywhere near anyone with a weapon unless she was properly attired.

Marissa spent the first few minutes of practice exchanging hugs with returning teammates, then helped new arrivals find equipment before she checked in with Erin, who was sitting by the sideline.

"Why don't we at least get you suited up, so you'll be all set if you decide you want to join tomorrow?"

Erin agreed, and by the time she had been fitted with all the necessary protective gear and had chosen one of the blunted weapons from the equipment closet, she had also agreed to change into her gym clothes and join them for warm-ups.

Much to Erin's relief, a good chunk of practice was devoted to safety rules, such as never fencing without a mask—"because your eye will explode on impact," according to Marissa—and then to proper posture and footwork.

"No matter how fast you are with your hands and your eyes, if you can't move your feet, you're a stationary target and you're going to get hit," Marissa said, taking over as team captain under the coach's stern gaze. "Also, if you don't watch your *en garde* posture, you'll not only be slow, but you can do serious damage to your knees, so do *not* complain when I make you do it over and over until everyone gets it right."

Such intense focus on the basics was kind of boring, but Tina had been right—Erin did enjoy the workout and the company of her teammates. *Her* teammates. By the end of practice, Erin had spoken to and learned the names of a dozen girls, who also knew her name and talked to her like a regular person.

At four o'clock, after they had all retreated from the center of the gym and stretched out what Erin knew were going to be intensely sore muscles, Marissa and another senior demonstrated what a real fencing bout could look like.

"Dana's mother is an Olympic fencer," one of the other girls told Erin. The older girl hadn't made any effort to speak to the newcomers on the team, spending any social moments chatting with girls she already knew.

Dana was good, but it was soon obvious that Marissa was holding back.

You don't know anything about this sport, Erin reminded herself. *How can you tell she's holding back? You're just biased because Marissa's your friend.*

Regardless, both fencers seemed excellent. Each movement was so tightly controlled and elegant the bout was beautiful to watch. The coach quickly got on Erin's nerves as she kept interrupting Marissa and Dana to ask them to repeat a certain move while she explained what it was useful for.

Near the end, Marissa seemed to uncoil. Suddenly, her movements were like silk, almost too fluid for Erin's gaze to follow, and Dana was on the defensive. Erin grinned, no longer caring *how* she had known that Marissa wasn't putting her all into the bout, but satisfied to see her impression confirmed.

That is someone who should be taken very seriously, Erin found herself thinking. *She could be dangerous.*

She started at the intrusive thought. Marissa, dangerous? Maybe as an opponent in a fencing match, but not in real life.

Erin's joy at watching the match was suddenly diminished, replaced by the same low level of anxiety that had kept her up the night before and the sleepiness that exercise and concentration had chased away for hours. Marissa and Dana were still wrapped up in their bout, but the coach had given everyone else permission to leave, and some of the other girls had already wandered off to change.

Erin approached the coach and, with a hand that trembled only a little, added her name and phone number to the team list. With the last of her energy and bravery gone, she hurried home.

Chapter 3

WHITE PILL, BLUE PILL, yellow pill, purple pill; it was like swallowing a rainbow every bedtime. Erin downed the evening's medication with a sports drink the neon orange of sweet-and-sour chicken glaze. Her homework was already done; she had checked her e-mail—all spam—and she had picked out her clothes for the next morning. That was for the best, since with any luck, her pretty colored pills would put her to sleep quickly that night.

She tried not to think about the facts that at least one of her medications was addictive and that taking such high levels of antipsychotic and antianxiety medication for so long could result in heart or liver failure.

She could ignore all that, because of that afternoon.

Despite how nervous she had been, she was glad that neither her therapist nor her father had discouraged her from accepting Marissa's invitation. She didn't think she had ever had a day go so well.

She crawled into bed, thinking about fencing, and chemistry, and *Romeo and Juliet,* and the nearly full moon that was pouring light across her floor.

Sleep came quickly, and later came dreams. . . .

. . . and waking in a strange place. Erin knew she wasn't home, because it was too dark to see anything, and her room at home had sheer curtains that let in enough light from outside that she could always see. More disconcerting was the fact that her head was tucked down against someone else's chest so she could feel him breathe and hear his steady, even heartbeat. One of his arms was around her waist, and the other was under her head.

"You awake?" he asked when she started to pull away from him.

Of course. She wasn't awake; that would explain it.

"I don't think so," she replied.

"Then go back to sleep," he suggested. "You were badly hurt. You need your rest."

She nodded, put her head back down, and went back to sleep. . . .

. . . and woke again, this time in the right place, to her alarm clock's wailing. She flailed at it, then stood and stumbled into the shower, lifting her face to the hot water to try to wake up completely.

Weird dreams the night before. One of them had

involved aliens and soy milk. The last one had been the most vivid. She had almost expected to wake up with someone holding her.

She had another rainbow of pills for breakfast, with a glass of water and a plate of scrambled eggs and toast with blackberry jelly.

She wondered what Marissa would think if she knew exactly who she had invited onto her team. This was not the first time the thought had crossed her mind, but it usually made her feel guilty. Today she found herself thinking that Marissa might be okay with it after all.

It was hard to imagine being completely accepted, though. Sometimes Erin wasn't even sure *she* knew who she was, though she knew a little too well who she could be without the medication and frequent therapy sessions.

Her mood continued to lift throughout the morning. She gave a triumphant report of her first day on a team to Tina and was thrilled to hear in English class that they were almost done with *Romeo and Juliet*. Her French teacher handed back their last essay, and Erin was even more excited about Marissa's A than her own. Erin didn't think she did *quite* as well on the chemistry exam that followed, but she didn't feel too bad about how it went, either.

Fencing warm-ups and stretches after school contributed to her sense of contentment, as did the friendly chatter among her teammates.

Then Marissa handed her a weapon.

"Erin, you're a natural!" Marissa praised her as they started going over not just footwork, but blade work.

Despite how tired her legs and weapon arm felt, the parries and lunges did seem to come naturally to her, as if she were remembering them, not learning them for the first time.

As Marissa and the coach demonstrated the eight fencing parries they would all eventually learn, not only did Erin know how to do them, but more unnerving, she knew what their uses would be if the team lived in a time and place where people fought serious battles with a blade. Granted, she could attribute her knowledge to her previous biology classes, but that didn't explain why she felt the need to mentally note which parry protected the heart, the throat, the liver, or—

Stop it! She chastised herself. *Fencing has practical roots, but it's just a sport now. A game.*

She was grateful when Marissa's attention was drawn away by a visitor. The coach frowned as Marissa apologized, removed her mask, and jogged across the gym to greet a middle-aged man Erin didn't know.

"Pair up, girls," the coach commanded. "I want you to take turns with a simple extension and parry four. If you're new to the team, try to work with one of the older girls."

Erin was paired with the senior she had watched Marissa spar with the day before. Dana approached the exercise with boredom and was obviously annoyed enough by it to put Erin on guard—especially after the coach came by, complimented Erin, and chastised her star fencer for lazy posture.

"You've got this," Dana announced abruptly. "Want to try something harder?"

"Aren't we supposed to—"

"This is a waste of time," Dana said. "The coach won't mind if we move on."

Erin had some doubts about that but shrugged anyway. "Okay," she said. "I don't—"

Without any more warning, Dana saluted her. Erin found herself parrying an attack before she had a chance to think about it. Her heart jumped into her throat, but she responded, mostly by instinct. Dana apparently took that as a cue to continue with a full-scale bout, setting Erin on the defensive . . . a position she didn't like at all.

For a few seconds, Erin struggled to watch what Dana was doing; Erin sloppily blocked attacks, barely avoiding a touch. Then she stopped thinking; she slipped into the white noise mind-set she often experienced when she was sleepy and drawing. Her body took over, remembering moves she couldn't possibly have seen, much less ever performed.

She could feel her muscles protesting, warning her that she was doing *damage* to herself, as the bout continued. She wasn't used to this kind of exertion. Deeper inside her, though, there was a voice saying, *Defend yourself. Attack. Win. Survive first, and you can lick your wounds later.*

Distantly, someone was shouting, but the world had narrowed to encompass only her and her opponent.

The spell was broken when someone threw something

between them—a wrestling mat, she realized as she jumped out of the way. Why . . . ?

She looked up and discovered that most of the team were watching them, including the coach, who looked impressed but less than pleased.

Erin had been oblivious to her physical state, focused only on her and her partner's weapons, but now she noticed that she was sweating and breathing heavily enough that she had to take a break or she would pass out or throw up or both. Some of the medication she was on was designed to prevent panic attacks by keeping her heart rate normal, which meant that her body went through more stress when she exercised than a normal person's would. Her doctors had taught her how to be careful and pace herself, but for however long the bout had gone on, she had been thinking of anything *but* caution.

Dana had lowered her weapon and turned to talk to the coach. Erin took a few steps back, pulled off her mask, and mumbled, "Drink," as she pushed past her teammates.

She leaned against the vending machine and fed it quarters while her thoughts from the match began to catch up with her. Thoughts containing words like 'danger' and 'defend yourself' and 'kill.'

She gagged and stumbled out the door. Fresh air would be good.

Marissa was standing near the parking lot, still talking to the man who had come to the gym. Now, however, she was as pale as a ghost. She asked a question, too quietly for Erin to hear, and the man nodded.

In response, Marissa let out a ragged scream. The man tried to put a hand on her arm, no doubt intending to be comforting, but Marissa pulled back, turned, and ran toward the path through the woods that the team had run for warm-ups.

Someone should go after her, Erin thought. Cursing, she dropped her water bottle and followed Marissa. She was supposed to be resting, but she had seen the expression on Marissa's face and feared what Marissa might do to herself if left alone.

Marissa outdistanced Erin almost immediately, and as soon as she was out of sight, Erin stumbled and collapsed, coughing and gagging. But when she heard Marissa let out a cry of anger and pain, she forced herself to her feet and continued, slowly, toward the sound.

Through the trees, she finally glimpsed Marissa. The petite girl was leaning forward against a large oak, her arms wrapped around its trunk. She seemed to be crying.

"Marissa?" Erin said softly.

Marissa looked up, and the despair on her face changed to fury. "I—" She broke off. "You . . . go away!"

"Marissa, please talk to me," Erin said. "I—"

Marissa snarled. "Erin, you've been a good friend, but right now I really need you to leave me alone."

Erin flinched but stood her ground. Maybe she was suffering from an excess of therapy, but she didn't intend to leave a friend alone in this kind of distress. She had seen too many people hospitalized as a result of their own actions.

"I think maybe you shouldn't *be* alone right now," she said.

Marissa didn't respond—not with words, at least.

Erin's vision wavered, and Marissa's body seemed to contort. Her skin rippled, gold and black bands crossing it, and her small, slender form seemed to fill out, expanding. Her black hair spread, becoming stripes. The hands that rested against the tree trunk thickened, becoming furred.

All this happened within seconds as Erin watched, choking for breath.

The tigress looked at Erin with a steady gaze just long enough for her to take a large step backward, and then with an animal scream it turned away. "Marissa" dragged her claws down the tree trunk, ripping through the bark and into the live wood beneath.

Erin continued to move away, not from the tiger, but from the spot where she knew a tiger *could not be.* It was all in her mind. In that moment, a rainbow of medication finally lost its battle against outright panic. Her heart rate jumped and she started to tremble, and finally, as she turned and fled, her body agreed with her. *Run! Flee! Get away!*

But how could you run from your own mind?

How could you run from being crazy?

At first she was running blind. She didn't want to return to the gym and face her own disturbing, violent thoughts. She certainly didn't want to face Marissa. She didn't know what she might do.

Finally, Erin curled up in a secluded spot at the edge of school. She swallowed one of the pills she kept on hand for panic attacks, then put her head down, called her father's cell phone, and told him to pick her up right away. He confirmed twice that she was okay, and asked if he needed to call 911, while in the background she could hear him grab his keys and start the car. She assured him that she would be fine . . . as long as he got there soon.

While she waited, she tried to think about *nothing*. She drew deep breaths, as she had been taught, counting the length of each exhalation to keep them slow and even. She had to stay calm. That was the only way to keep the monster at bay.

Chapter 4

ERIN WOKE ONCE AGAIN in a dark room, but this time it didn't feel like a dream. She thought she had fallen asleep in her father's car, which was unusual. The only times she remembered blacking out like that . . .

Where was she?

What had she done?

She pushed herself up and then gasped: Her body ached. She shoved her hair out of her face and groped blindly for the edge of the bed and, from there, for a lamp. She needed light. She needed—

Don't freak out again, Erin. Deep breaths. She consciously controlled her breathing as she located a bedside table.

Instead of finding a lamp, she touched a small box, maybe for jewelry. A . . . *pair of handcuffs?* A little less carefully and a little more frantically, she searched further, and then bit back a scream as she grabbed something sharp, cutting her hand.

She recoiled, hugging her injured hand to her chest, and ended up in the middle of the dark room. She shuffled forward, her uninjured hand in front of her face, until she found the wall and breathed a sigh of relief.

The relief was short-lived. In that moment, a door behind her opened, letting in a stream of muted but appreciated light and a man she had never seen before.

He looked a little older than Erin—maybe a college student—though he had a quality about him that made Erin think he was older than that. His skin was caramel-bronze, and his short, tousled hair was the color of good coffee beans. What didn't match were his silver-and-blue eyes, which reminded her of a blue jay dipped in mercury. He didn't look like anyone she remembered ever knowing, but at the same time he seemed familiar. Those *eyes,* currently focused on her with what appeared to be concern, seemed like eyes she must have stared into for hours, once upon a time in another life.

Maybe she had.

This thought made Erin's skin crawl.

"Where am I?" she asked in a voice so muted she barely recognized it as her own.

"In your room, in your Sète home." He looked worried now. "Do you remember how you got here?"

Sète? She had never heard of it.

"What state?"

Now he looked confused. "Shevaun, why don't you sit down? You were badly hurt. This is the first time you've been conscious in days, and I think you're still disoriented."

"What did you call me?" But Erin already knew. She knew because she had heard the name before. It was written in all her records.

"Shevaun, sit down—"

He moved to touch her arm and she jerked back.

"I've got to go. I have to leave, *now.*"

"Shevaun—"

"Don't call me that!"

As she remembered what he had said, she demanded, "Hurt—how? How was I hurt? What did I do?"

Erin didn't want to go back to the ward, to lockdowns and body searches and waking up in restraints, but wasn't this worse? At least when she woke up in isolation, she knew where she was and who she was with. *Who was this man and what had she done?*

"Calm down," he was saying, but she couldn't. She knew what "Shevaun" was capable of; any friend of that woman's was no friend of hers. Erin needed only to glance at the bedside table—and the handcuffs, the knife, and the bottle of wine there—to know that.

The man reached for her again. This time she shoved him, discovering in her panic a strength she hadn't known she possessed, until suddenly the stranger was sprawled full-length on the ground. Seizing her advantage, she dashed past him, only to slam into a tall, slender girl with unruly blond hair. The girl stumbled a bit but managed to keep her footing and grab Erin's arm.

"Shevaun, you're awake!"

The girl's glowing happiness was quickly replaced by confusion as the man Erin had run from said, "Brittany, don't let her past you. Something's wrong."

"Something *is* wrong," Erin said swiftly as the man moved up behind her and grasped one of her wrists in each hand. "I don't know what I've told you, but I'm not who you think I am. And I need to get home, right away."

"You *are* home," Brittany said.

"No, I'm *not*—"

"Brittany, why don't you give us some privacy?" the man asked.

Brittany nodded. "I'll wait in the parlor, in case you need me."

Parlor? Who has a parlor in this day and age?

Apparently, Shevaun did, along with this old-money Victorian-style bedroom, with a four-poster bed, an Oriental carpet, and honest-to-god oil paintings on the walls.

Not to mention handcuffs and a knife, and a man Erin had never met.

"Please," she whispered, "let me call my father. He'll explain."

The man holding her didn't reply. Instead, he pulled them both down onto the bed, where he spooned against her back, pinning one of her arms underneath her and keeping her other wrist in his hand, against her shoulder. He was gentle, but Erin knew that he was perfectly ready to roll forward and pin her more thoroughly if she struggled.

"Let's start over," he said, in a tone that was oh-so-careful. "My name is Adjila. I am in love with Shevaun, so you can be assured that I won't hurt you, that I have a vested interest in figuring out what is going on, and that I am not going to let you out of this house until I am confident you are safe. Even if you were making sense to me, I would attempt to discourage you from leaving, due to your current physical condition, which you would *notice,* if you would calm down enough to recognize that you are still injured."

Aware that she wouldn't be able to get up until he let her, Erin forced herself to relax. As she did so, she confirmed what he had said: her whole body hurt. The pain seemed most focused in her gut and her ribs, but everything ached, as if she had either had a serious flu or taken an equally serious beating. She was sure she had pulled a lot of muscles fencing and then chasing after Marissa, but this was a different kind of pain. Deeper.

"Okay, I've calmed down," she said. "Would you let go of me now?"

"So you can run off?" Adjila guessed, correctly. "No."

"Actually, because it creeps me out to have a guy I don't

know snuggling with me," she snapped. It was her secondary reason, but that didn't make it less true.

She felt him flinch, and an unexpected wave of pity washed over her. He had claimed to love Shevaun. She was about to tell him that Shevaun didn't exist.

"If it would make you less uneasy," he said, "I can tie you down instead."

She drew a deep breath. "I don't want to be tied up."

"I didn't think so. Now, if you aren't Shevaun, why don't you let me know who you *are*?"

"I've been trying to—"

"So do it," he snapped. Then it was his turn to take one of those deep, calming breathes before he asked, "What's your name?"

She gave him that and more. "Erin Misrahe. I live in Massachusetts. I'm sixteen." She hoped that that might make him back off a little, since he was obviously older and they apparently had some kind of serious relationship.

"Do you often wander around in other people's brains . . . Erin?" he asked, hesitating only a little on the name.

It was a weird way to put it, but she knew what he meant, and tried to answer honestly with words she never expected to say to a complete stranger—one who wasn't some kind of health care professional, anyway.

"I'm schizophrenic," she admitted softly as she tried to remember Tina's words on the subject. *It's a disease, Erin; it's not who you are. It's not your fault. It's not something you chose, or something you should blame yourself for, or feel ashamed of. All you can choose is to keep fighting it.* "I was diagnosed when I was a little kid. Add to that a dissociative identity disorder, and you get however I met you and got here. I've been symptom-free for almost two years . . . until now."

Until now. For the first time in her life, things had been going well and she had begun to feel hope. She had a life, finally—or she had, until she'd woken up that day with a stranger who knew her by another name.

"Are we . . ." She fought back unwanted tears. Why did this have to happen, now of all times? "Have we—I mean, do we . . ."

She trailed off, and without releasing her wrist, he squeezed her with the arm draped over her waist.

"We've been together for . . . a while."

"We met before this?"

He hesitated, apparently evaluating her question before he answered, "We met years ago."

Years?

When?

She had run away often in the past, while her other persona was in charge. When it had happened, Erin had woken up hours or days later, often restrained, with nothing but a black block in her memory to explain the lost time. She had rarely managed to get away and still be free when she came to her senses, but it had happened.

Erin had not known that she had ever gotten wherever Shevaun had intended, but apparently she had. She had somehow formed a whole other life. How worried had these people been during the past two years, while Erin was symptom-free, if Shevaun was as real to them as Erin was to her father and the ward?

"I'm sorry," she whispered without meaning to. Sorry for the pain she must have put these strangers through— and sorry that she would do whatever it took to kill "Shevaun" for good. She felt some pity for this man, but she didn't love him. She didn't know or care about the girl he had called Brittany. She would hurt them if she had to, if it got her life back.

Adjila seemed to make a decision. He said, "Erin, I'm going to walk with you to the bathroom. You are going to look in the mirror and tell me whether the face you see there is the one you are used to seeing. If the answer is yes, we will go get the phone, and I will let you call . . . your father, you said?"

"Yeah."

"If I let you up, are you going to attack me again?"

She shook her head. He was going to let her call her father. That was all she needed to confirm her identity and find a way home.

They stood up. Adjila let her walk on her own, but he never put more than a single small step between them. They passed through another door from the bedroom, into an enormous bathroom.

The large Jacuzzi-style tub was black marble, and the shelves on each side held cranberry-scented candles and an assortment of soaps and other necessities. The floor was creamy white tile, and the counter was more black marble, covered with a scattering of objects that ranged from a mahogany-handled hairbrush and a tube of lipstick to an antique-looking but obviously razor-sharp dagger.

Finally, Erin lifted her gaze to the mirror. Where she expected to find short brown hair and hazel eyes, she instead saw tousled auburn hair and eyes as dark as jet, so pure the pupils could not be differentiated from the iris.

"That's not me," she gasped. She ran into Adjila as she tried to step backward.

"I didn't think it would be," he replied as he wrapped his arms around her waist, pinning hers at her side. Still speaking slowly and quietly, as if to tame some wild animal, he said, "Shevaun . . ." He had gone back to using that name. God! How she hated that name! "I have known you, continuously, for a great many years. We have been *together*"—he held her more tightly when she started to struggle—"for almost as long."

"No," she whimpered, and then repeated more strongly, "No," before finally shouting it. "No! *No!* You *bastard*!" She kicked at his shins, fought and shouted and squirmed and cursed. "You're messing with me. You're—you're—" But there was that face in the mirror, with those black eyes, which stared back at her, wide and frightened.

"Shevaun, calm down!"

"Don't call me that, you *sick, twisted, son of a*—"

He spun her around and roughly pinned her against the wall.

"Erin," he said, in a tone that was no longer gentle, "calm down, or I will knock you out and simply pray that the next time you open your eyes, the right person looks out of them."

"Get your hands *off me*!"

This time he lifted her and half carried, half dragged her, still struggling, back toward the bed. "You're going to hurt yourself," he warned. She landed a lucky elbow in his rib cage and he gasped, dropping her. She landed hard on her hip. "Or you're going to hurt me," he coughed. "You don't know your own strength."

"Good," she spat, scuttling back and jumping to her feet again. "Come and get it."

He did, too quickly for her to follow. Without quite knowing how he'd managed it, she found herself pinned on her stomach on the bed, with one of her arms twisted painfully up behind her back to hold her in place.

"Stop this!" he ordered.

"Not. Freaking. Likely."

She recalled the handcuffs only when he shifted his weight to grab them. She tried to throw him off, but Adjila was quick and he knew what he was doing—which shouldn't have surprised her, given what she had seen so far in these rooms.

Erin did the only thing she could think of as this stranger cuffed her wrists behind her back: she screamed bloody murder.

Adjila thumped her against the bed, knocking the wind

out of her, at the same time that the door opened and another girl Erin didn't know—a brunette, this time—poked her head in.

"Everything okay in here?" the new girl asked.

"*Nothing* is okay in here," Erin shouted as soon as she managed to take another breath. "Call the police! I've been—"

Adjila shifted his weight just enough to push her breath out again and quiet her as he said, gritting his teeth, "We're fine."

"Okay." The girl stepped back and closed the door without another word.

"Erin," Adjila ordered, his tone now vicious, "shut up. No one can hear you except Brittany, Iana, and me, and they're going to listen to *me* until you start acting more like *you*. Now, I don't want to hurt you, but I will if I have to . . . especially if you manage to break another one of my ribs."

"You'd hurt your precious Shevaun?" Erin said, challenging him.

"I know how much your body can heal from, and she knows how much damage it can inflict," he snarled. "She'll forgive me for defending myself as soon as she . . . gets back. And you had better hope that she *is* back by the next time those pretty black eyes open, because otherwise, I am going to have to get creative, and you probably aren't going to enjoy that. So shut your mouth, shut your eyes, and go to sleep, or I swear to Heaven, Hell, and all the worlds between, I will give you good reason to scream."

Erin wasn't crazy enough to challenge this man who kept weapons and handcuffs so close at hand. She shut her eyes and her mouth and silently prayed she would wake up in the hospital.

Chapter 5

"PLEASE, MR. MISRAHE, it's incredibly important. Erin saw something, and I need to explain it."

Thank you, god, Erin thought as she woke to the sound of Marissa's anxious voice outside her bedroom. She felt a little hungover from the antianxiety meds, but she wasn't bruised, cuffed, or anywhere she wasn't supposed to be, and a quick examination revealed that her hair was still short and dark brown.

Could it really have been nothing more than a fear-induced nightmare? She had been so scared waiting for her father to arrive that it was very possible her brain had given that chronic terror a form.

One little hallucination didn't mean a serious relapse. During the past two years, she had occasionally seen auras or had outright auditory or visual hallucinations, but they went away eventually. She had probably brought this one on by pushing herself too hard at practice and then chasing after Marissa.

There was actually a spring in her step—albeit a slightly groggy one—as she left her bedroom and walked into the hallway, where her father was standing with Marissa.

"Erin, do you feel up to having a visitor?" her father asked, the worry in his eyes mostly hidden in his voice.

She smiled and hugged him, both because she wanted to and because it would confirm to him who she was. The identity confusion from her nightmare, unfortunately, had come from real life. "I'm okay, Dad."

He let out a relieved breath.

Erin wondered if the terror and anxiety she felt during her nightmare were what "Shevaun" felt whenever she woke up in Erin's life. No wonder Shevaun had always been violent. Erin wondered if the dream had been inspired by the actual created memories of her alter. Shevaun had a life and a history that, though entirely the product of Erin's schizophrenic imagination, was as real to Shevaun as Erin's own past was to Erin. Erin had never been able to remember that other life, and Shevaun had rarely been cooperative in discussing it. Now Erin made a mental note to ask her father and Tina if they had ever heard her mention Adjila, Brittany, or . . . Laura, Lana? She couldn't remember the last name he had said.

She hadn't exactly been paying attention at the time, and now she wished she had been. She wished she could have gone with the dream instead of panicking, so that she'd know more, but even the limited amount she remembered had to be some kind of breakthrough. Tina had often implied that if they knew more about Erin's alter, they might be able to learn something about why she'd been created. Severe dissociation was usually the result of some kind of horrendous childhood trauma or long-term abuse, neither of which Erin had suffered, which was why Shevaun had always been such a mystery. One therapist had tried to pin it on misplaced guilt for her mother's death in childbirth, but though Erin was sad not to have known her mother, her father had always made sure she knew it wasn't her fault.

"Erin?" Marissa asked, snapping Erin free of her racing thoughts.

"Sorry," Erin said. "Spaced for a second. What time is it?"

"Quarter past seven at night," her father replied. "You slept a few hours."

She wasn't normally scheduled to see Tina on Wednesdays, but Erin knew that her primary therapist would want to hear about this. "Dad, could you call Tina for me?" she asked, keeping the request vague so that she could explain to Marissa in her own way. "Tell her I think it's good news, but I'd really like to see her as soon as possible."

"Sure. I told her I would call when you woke up, anyway. Will you two be okay if I leave you alone?"

"We're good." Erin was so relieved not to be in restraints that she felt like she could handle anything. "Thanks, Dad."

Erin and Marissa retreated to her room, where Marissa

sat in the desk chair and Erin perched on the edge of her quilted comforter.

While Marissa looked around the room, Erin felt a renewed sense of appreciation for the sparse but precious possessions that marked this space as her own.

There were four posters taped to the wall, mostly of surrealist art, which Erin had been introduced to by a roommate in her last hospital. On her desk was a wax reproduction of *Orpheus and Eurydice* by Auguste Rodin. And in the daytime, sunlight streamed through a circle of stained glass that was meant to mimic a rose window, casting streaks of color across her thick white carpet.

Her walls were a bold shade of pine green, and none of the furniture in her room was bolted down.

The little things in life were what Erin appreciated.

Marissa's silence was not one of those little things. Erin decided that one of them had to start, and it might as well be her.

"I'm sorry I flipped out," she said, "especially when you were obviously upset. The last thing you needed to worry about was *me.*"

Marissa shook her head. "Don't apologize. You had every right to freak, after what you saw."

That wasn't quite the reaction Erin had expected. Now she wanted to know what really had happened that afternoon for Marissa to feel that Erin's reaction was justified. Several horrific possibilities instantly sprang to mind.

"What do you mean? Is everything all right?" Erin

would never forgive herself for running away instead of helping if Marissa had been hurt.

Marissa's gaze dropped, and she bit her lip.

"I . . . got some bad news. But I should never have . . ." She trailed off. "Erin, I don't even know where to start."

"Do you want to talk about the . . . news?" Erin was far more concerned about Marissa's well-being than her own now.

Marissa started to shake her head, then stopped. Tears filled her eyes, but she blinked them away rapidly. Erin reached out, and Marissa grasped her hand tightly.

"It's not your fault," Marissa said. "I believe that, really I do. It's *not* your fault."

"Um, okay," Erin said slowly. *Oh, god, what had she done?* Had she dissociated after all, before her father arrived? Had she hurt someone? Had she hurt *Marissa*? Had she—

"My brother is dead," Marissa blurted out. "That's what the man who came to see me had to say. My brother, and one of my cousins."

"Oh, god," Erin whispered. Horribly, the first emotion to hit her was relief; she hadn't done it. Guilt quickly followed; how could she possibly be grateful about *anything* when Marissa had just lost two members of her family? "I'm so, *so* sorry," she said. "And thank you, for coming to see if I'm okay, but really, you shouldn't have to—"

Marissa shook her head. "Never mind me for a minute," she said. "I should never have responded the way I did in front of you. I was just so *angry*, and I took it out on you."

Erin remembered Marissa yelling at her to leave, but nothing worth this level of concern. "It's okay. I ran off mostly because of my own issues, not because of anything you said."

"Still, I should—"

"Marissa, there's something I have to tell you," Erin interrupted. "You have to understand that I don't even *know* what I saw, because I . . ." She didn't want to make the conversation all about her when Marissa obviously needed comfort more, but Marissa needed to know the truth so she would stop blaming herself for Erin's behavior. Erin stared at the colored lights cast on the floor by the rose window as she explained. "I see things sometimes, things that aren't there. It hasn't happened in a while, but sometimes anxiety or fatigue will bring on an episode."

Marissa blinked, but that was her only reaction, as if she were too emotionally drained even to feel surprise. "You're prone to hallucinations?"

Forcing the words out, Erin said bluntly, "I'm *prone* to outright psychosis. I spent most of my childhood institutionalized, and then spent the last two years with nearly constant supervision so my doctors could make sure I didn't relapse. I've finally stabilized enough—or, to tell the whole truth, they've finally stabilized my medication enough—that I've been almost completely symptom-free for the last eighteen months, which is why I'm enrolled in your school. This is the first time I've been in public school since first grade."

She lifted her gaze, then looked away again when she saw exactly what she had feared: horror and pity.

Marissa struggled to rally. "Things have been normal for almost two years?"

Erin nodded miserably. "Like I said, sometimes when I get too tired or I'm under a lot of stress, things get funky, but I haven't had a major episode since March twelfth, last year." She was half begging, and she knew it. *Please,* she wanted to say, *trust me. I'm okay now. Believe me.* "So, you see, it wasn't your fault. Whatever you said or did, I know it wasn't personal, and my reaction wasn't anything you could have predicted. You were upset, and—"

"You remember the exact date?" Without waiting for a response, Marissa sighed. "It must have been really tough to pull yourself up from that. I'm sure it took a lot of courage."

Erin looked up again with a self-deprecating smile. "You don't have to humor me."

"I'm not. I'm just imagining how hard . . . It *does* sound like I'm patronizing you, doesn't it?" Marissa said. "I don't mean to. I'm impressed."

"Impressed that I'm crazy?"

"Impressed that you've kept fighting." Marissa instantly corrected her. The horror and pity were gone, replaced by determination. "Change has to be hard when you've spent so much time struggling to know what's real."

Erin wasn't sure if it was healthy for Marissa to avoid the subject of her own loss, but Erin was no therapist. She was just grateful Marissa was being so understanding. "It was scary for a while, wondering if I would wake up one day and realize that I only dreamed I was going to a real school. That must sound so weird to someone who has always been in school. I never thought I'd be able to. It was hard to accept that—well, like you said, that things could change so drastically."

Erin's father ducked his head in just then. "Erin, Tina says she can see you tomorrow morning, but her only free hour is during your English class."

"That's fine." She could afford to miss that one. "Thanks, Dad." After he left, she added, "Tina's my therapist."

Marissa nodded. "All that doubting . . . it sounds terrifying."

Erin shrugged, acknowledging the truth, but not wanting to dwell on it further.

Marissa moved to sit next to Erin and put an arm over her shoulders. "I'm sorry I treated you badly yesterday when you came after me," she said, once more.

"You do *not* need to apologize for that," Erin insisted.

"I'm still sorry," Marissa said. "And I promise not to do it again. You tried to comfort me, even at risk to yourself. In my book that makes you a friend, and I don't give up my friends. For anyone. Will you be back in school tomorrow, after your appointment?"

Relieved, Erin nodded. "I should be. Are you going to be okay?"

Marissa nodded sharply. "If you're up to fencing practice, I hear you're a hell of a fencer," she said. "If you're not, I'll stop pressuring you. Whatever you need."

"Thanks. Marissa, if there's anything I can do—"

"No," Marissa snapped, then bit her lip. "Really. I'll be fine. I have a kind of support group I go to. They took me in when—never mind. Someday maybe I'll introduce you to them, but you've got enough on your plate right now." She seemed to realize she was rambling, and she stopped to compose herself. "Thanks for telling me about your past, Erin, for trusting me."

Unable to understand, much less reply to, some of Marissa's disjointed words, Erin instead forced a light tone. "The other option was a really good lie, but 'compulsive liar' was full the day I registered for crazy school."

Chapter 6

SHEVAUN WOKE UP with her wrists cuffed, her ankles tied together, and a solid ache throughout her body that seemed to originate at her stomach and chest. To top it off, her bedroom door was open, though she always slept with it closed for privacy.

She tested the cuffs and the ropes and couldn't get free of either, which meant Adjila had probably put them there; only a Triste witch had the magic necessary to make bonds a vampire could not break. Adjila had a wicked sense of humor, but this wasn't his style of practical joke. Instead of trying to find her own way out of the unexpected restraints, she called, "Someone want to explain how I ended up the Christmas goose?"

Adjila appeared in the doorway instantly, as she had known he would. He wouldn't wander far with her in this kind of position.

"Shevaun?" His voice was unusually hesitant, and the uncertainty in his silver-struck eyes was so uncharacteristic that it made her smile.

"If you're expecting to find someone else tied up on your bed, we've got to have a talk."

He crossed the room with swift strides and collapsed next to her on the bed, one hand holding a key to the cuffs while the other twined in her hair to lift her head so he could kiss her.

She might have teased him for being so hasty, but she could taste the lingering fear on his lips and feel his relief in the press of his body. The moment her hands were free, she wrapped an arm around his waist to hold him close. She felt instantly that he was exhausted and burned out, and she wondered how long he had been babysitting her. When had he last slept, or fed?

Eventually, he broke away, and she took the opportunity to say, "The last thing I remember is walking down by the canal. How did I end up bound in my own bed?"

"Do you remember anything else?" he asked, pressing her.

She tried, but her memory skipped from moonlight on the water to waking up here. "*Rien*. Nothing."

"You were attacked," Adjila said. "There were six hunters. Between the whole half-dozen, they didn't have the sense to fill a brandy snifter, but they got in a lucky shot."

As he spoke, the memory came to her. "I was walking by the canal, and I noticed our little friends trying to stalk me. I circled around to get to the leader, but I only saw five of them." She tried to remember more, but everything went dark after she reached the leader. Someone must have been watching his back.

"The sixth one had a shotgun loaded with buckshot," Adjila said.

"He *shot* me?" That was just tacky. What ever happened to classy mercenaries? Even assassins could be suave. But *buckshot*? Art had gone out the window the day black powder had been invented.

"If it makes you feel any better, he killed his leader in the process," Adjila offered.

She grinned. "Idiot, playing with fire. So, I took a chestful of buckshot, which I imagine is what threw me off my game for a few moments. Then what?"

"Two of the hunters were shapeshifters. Somehow they got their hands on firestone, but it wasn't very powerful, and they had a little trouble locating your heart. Brittany and Iana did a number on the group while I worked on healing you. Unfortunately, the poison was already deep enough in your system that I had to suppress your power to draw it out. That's why you slept for so long."

She snuggled closer to Adjila. Most vampires knew very little about Triste witches and their abilities, which Shevaun thought was foolish, since Tristes were among the few species on Earth intrinsically *dangerous* to her kind. Of course, unlike Shevaun, most vampires had not had a Triste lover even for a night, much less for nearly five centuries. The breeds tended not to get along.

Shevaun's choice in partner had gravely disappointed

Theron, the vampire who had given her this life the night the moon was eclipsed and the great Byzantine Empire fell. Fortunately, it wasn't Theron's style to try to rule her, so he had chosen to ignore her relationship with Adjila instead of arguing about it.

"Did you save anyone for me?" She pouted. Six hunters, and she didn't get to kill *one*.

"We kept the owner of the shotgun cuffed next to the bed for a couple of days in case you woke up hungry, but he got lippy and Brittany ate him."

"That girl's feisty." Shevaun smiled. The members of her surrogate family were all independent, free-spirited, and charmingly violent. Brittany was an absolute sweetheart, the kind of girl who could give Little Orphan Annie some competition, right up until the moment she bared her fangs.

Focusing on the present, Shevaun said, "But a little spat with hunters wouldn't worry you so much, and it wouldn't end with me tied up."

Adjila looked troubled again as he detailed exactly what had happened from the moment a stranger had first invaded Shevaun's mind until she had woken up as herself again a few hours before dawn that day.

Shevaun did not breathe quickly when enraged, and her heart did not pound; neither of those things had happened since the day she'd died, hundreds of years before. She did not tremble or curse or shout. She simply contemplated, silently, what they should do.

"Massachusetts, the girl said?" she asked.

Adjila nodded.

Shevaun stood up, reached down just long enough to untie her ankles, and then stretched, feeling her spine lengthen and her body wake from its long rest.

"I suppose that means we're going to America again," she announced after she had twisted left and right to stretch out her back. "It's just as well; I'm bored of Sète."

They had spent upwards of two months in France this time, which was about as long as Shevaun was ever content to settle anywhere—and about as long as they could stay before they attracted serious hunters, like the ones who had attacked her with their nasty firestone.

The bloodred crystal of firestone was saturated with power from the strongest Triste witches. Only the wealthiest hunters could afford firestone of any quality, which was a good thing, since in its purer form it would have killed Shevaun long before Adjila arrived. As it was, if Adjila had not been able to remove the poison from her blood, it would have lingered in her system for months or even years, feeding on her power and leaving her weak.

Yes, it was time to leave France anyway. Shevaun had hoped to spend some time in China next, but she could stand a detour to the States first. It had been five or six years since she had spent more than a night on that side of the ocean.

"I'll make the arrangements," Adjila replied.

"First, we both need to hunt," Shevaun said. "Let's enjoy

the fine French cuisine one last time before shipping off to the New World, shall we?"

Adjila's lingering, slightly wicked smile returned, and he pulled her close and kissed her. "As my lady wishes, of course."

"I'm sure the girls have been as worried and cooped up here as you have been," she said. "Let's make it a family dinner."

Adjila shrugged but didn't argue as Shevaun groomed herself, dressed, and then stepped into the parlor, where she was immediately greeted by "her" girls.

A tiny blond waif with wide black eyes instantly launched herself at Shevaun.

In her mortal life, Brittany had been raised in an orphanage. She had been changed to a vampire when she was only fourteen, an age at which many wouldn't even survive the process, and then abandoned by her creator within a week. Whether he had been taken by a hunter's blade or simply changed his mind about his new fledgling, none of them knew. Almost two centuries ago Shevaun had found Brittany working in a human sweatshop, barely surviving as a vampire and hardly aware of what she was, with her skin filthy and her hair shorn to keep it from the machinery.

These days, Brittany's long wheat hair hung wild to her waist, occasionally streaked with blood after one of her hunts. Despite her radiant, innocent smile, which could brighten the darkest day, she could be one of the most vicious creatures Shevaun had ever seen.

Shevaun caught Brittany, returning her exuberant embrace while Iana—Brittany's "sister"—looked on patiently. Like Brittany, Iana had been an orphan both in the human world and in the vampiric one. A slender young woman of Irish descent, she had been changed in 1612 in London, where she had lived almost entirely alone for seven decades, hiding from everything, before Shevaun had saved her from a hunter's blade.

"We were worried about you," Iana said once Shevaun had put Brittany down again. "What happened?"

"We're still trying to figure that out," Shevaun answered. "In the meantime, we're going back to America tomorrow, so let's have some fun tonight."

She did not need to ask the girls if they minded traveling. Home was wherever they were together. That was what mattered.

Brittany grinned and grabbed Iana's hand. "The hunters *are* gone. We should make the best of their absence," Iana said practically.

The four of them tumbled onto the dark predawn streets, Brittany and Iana still holding hands like sisters, and Adjila and Shevaun trailing them. Despite the early hour, the streets were never empty in such a popular tourist area.

"Ah, *l'amour*," Adjila said, nodding to a couple exchanging deep stares and soft smiles while nestled together on a bench. "Nothing sweeter."

When Adjila put a hand on the young man's arm, the

man looked up with an annoyed expression at first but quickly became dazed and pliant. Shevaun watched, amazed even after many years of hunting by Adjila's side, as he whispered a few words into the young woman's ear, instantly transforming the expression on her face from hostile confusion to the same peaceful adoration that already marked her partner's.

Unlike Shevaun and the girls, Adjila did not need to feed on blood to survive. As a Triste witch, he could pull power from a mortal—or, for that matter, from a vampire or a witch or a shapeshifter—through touch.

Brittany and Iana didn't feel the need to be nearly so subtle. They exchanged a look, then placed themselves in the path of a group of drunken American tourists. Iana smiled at them, her soft, cool expression simultaneously inviting and disturbing. Shevaun saw Adjila look up and flex his power just before Iana wrapped her arms around one of the young men's waists, snuggled close, and set her teeth into his throat.

With the Triste's magic veiling the area, any other humans passing by were blithely unaware of the monsters in their midst, even as Brittany pounced on one of the other boys. Shevaun heard the crunch of a bone crushed in Brittany's slender hands, but she had already turned to her own prey. Snuggling on the bench with Adjila and the infatuated young couple, she gently pierced the woman's throat.

Shevaun was content to feed more than once that night

rather than killing this young couple. Adjila followed her lead, and when they left, the lovers were both asleep, leaning against each other.

Shevaun and Adjila finally curled up in bed to sleep as the new day brightened. It was a short night for all of them—usually they would have woken midafternoon and stayed out dancing until well past dawn—but recent events and several nights without sustenance had taken their toll.

Adjila kissed Shevaun good night, a chaste brush of lips on her forehead, which she responded to with a kiss at the hollow of his throat. The exchange meant more between them than a more intimate embrace would have. After all, he could have killed her in an instant with the same contact, just as she could have returned the gesture by ripping his throat out instead of kissing it.

The touches were a ritual between them. They spoke of love, trust, and commitment—the three things neither of them had known in their human lives and few of their kinds allowed themselves in immortality.

Of course, few people had the power to protect even themselves in the world that crept out of the shadows after dark, much less the power to afford themselves luxuries like trust and faith.

Shevaun and Adjila could. Idiotic buckshot-wielding would-be hunters aside, not many people dared challenge their family, because those who did always lost. She wondered if the group with the rifle had targeted her for any particular reason, but decided she had probably just crossed "their" territory. She was well known among vampires and among hunters; she had never made much of an attempt to hide or to pacify anyone, whether she was in the mood to paint with oils or blood.

In the warm foggy zone between waking and sleep, her thoughts turned once more to the girl who had called herself Erin.

What was she? A witch, maybe even another Triste, who had managed something Adjila had not even conceived? Adjila was more than a half millennium old, but even he admitted that there were skills among his kind that he did not understand. Or perhaps she was one of the many rarer breeds of immortal or shaman or spirit?

According to Adjila, the girl had claimed to suffer from some kind of human madness, which could mean anything. She could have some psychic ability and not know it; if she had been raised by humans, that would account for her thinking herself mad. Or she might really, truly be insane. The mad were often capable of things a "sane" human could not attempt or survive.

The only thing Shevaun knew for certain was that this girl had been in Shevaun's mind and body. Shevaun had been violated, and this Erin was the one who had done it— and intentional or not, what had been done once could be done again. Adjila certainly knew how to win a fight, but Shevaun was superior by far in terms of raw strength, and a vampire could heal in minutes wounds that would kill a Triste outright. He had said that Erin seemed unaware of her own destructive potential in this body, but Shevaun couldn't help imagining what Erin might have done to Adjila or the girls if she had known of it.

It didn't matter if the girl was mad or sane, innocent or guilty; she was a threat to this family, and *that* meant she had to be destroyed.

Chapter 7

IT WAS ALMOST FIVE in the morning in Massachusetts. Shevaun had to sleep soon, she knew, but she had been suffering from a restlessness she hadn't been able to control since they had arrived in Boston.

Brittany and Iana had curled up together and gossiped as they'd drifted off to sleep hours ago, and Adjila had gone to New Hampshire to tell his creator, Pandora, that he was back—not just in the country, but in territory that she claimed as hers.

Under different circumstances, Shevaun's first day in Massachusetts would have included a trip to Boston, to take in the history, the culture, and the flavor of a land that had shocked the world in 1776 by declaring that those "United Colonies are, and of Right ought to be Free and Independent States." Shevaun had been in Spain when the news had reached her, and had been absolutely amazed. Americans—what a fascinating breed.

Today, though, the city's soul did not call to her. Neither did the museums. No, today she was drawn to a town she had no name for, to find a person whose face she did not know. She tried to walk the city streets and enjoy the environment, but as she passed an Internet café, she found herself pausing outside the door. She passed by it twice before following the compulsion to go inside.

The young man behind the counter smiled at her in a hesitant way as he handed her a guest account card and a chai latte. She certainly did not need the drink, but she enjoyed the spicy scent almost as much as she enjoyed the smell of the young man's blood beneath his skin. The latter had a rich aroma that indicated that the boy was a little more than human, which didn't surprise Shevaun; shapeshifters and witches had interbred with humans in this country for centuries, often leaving offspring with no idea of their heritage. Sometimes that legacy revealed itself as power later in life, but many of those mutts never knew anything, even as they passed on their genes to their children.

Shevaun returned the smile. Maybe later.

Though Shevaun still appreciated old-fashioned luxuries, she was not lost in this fast-paced modern day, as many vampires let themselves become. As long as she was here, maybe she could find something about Erin online.

Erin Misrahe was sixteen, so she would probably not be listed under her own name. According to Adjila, she had referred only to her father, not her parents, which made Shevaun think she lived with him alone.

Experimenting with many possible spellings, Shevaun still found only a small handful of Misrahes in Massachusetts that were attached to male first names. She jotted them down, trying not to be distracted by the young man behind the counter. She had not regained all her strength, and the way he was watching her—with a fascination that said it would be easy to convince him to go somewhere more private—was simply too tempting.

With a cell phone she had swiped from the belt of a careless traveler on the plane, she began to try the numbers she had found. The second phone call she made met with success, in the form of an answering machine.

A young woman's recorded voice announced, "You have reached the Misrahe residence. Peter and Erin aren't here right—"

Shevaun hung up and memorized the relevant address.

"Excuse me?"

She looked up to find the cashier standing next to her. "Yes?"

"I'm sorry to bother you, but I'm sure I know you from somewhere."

Shevaun's creator had once said that her beauty was "as if God used the fires of the heart of the earth to paint" her. The boy's approach was not the worst pickup line she had ever heard.

She took an instant to debate, then decided that this was hardly a good time to confront Erin. She needed to rest, and of course, she needed to feed.

And God, with his palette of fire, had just delivered dinner.

She left the smitten young man unconscious in a chair behind the counter. He would wake perhaps a little faint but otherwise fine; he would not remember approaching her and would feel no adverse effects from their contact. Even the twin marks of her fangs on his neck had healed by the time she put him down. He would probably assume he had dozed off, as she imagined one occasionally would when working the predawn shift at such a place.

Inspired by the pleasant repast, Shevaun spent a few hours distractedly exploring the city while she waited for most of the human world to wake and begin their day. Once she started seeing school buses, and children disappeared into their classrooms, she was literally at Erin's home in the blink of an eye. Triste witches like Adjila might have fancy magics that she would never understand, but none of those meant as much to Shevaun as her vampiric ability to travel from place to place with the speed of thought.

Now, as she paced outside Erin Misrahe's empty home, she thought, *You invade my life; let's see what you keep in yours.*

The front lawn was neat, simple, with what would probably become a garden when fall plantings sprouted in the spring. The garage was free of clutter, with just a

well-organized box of yard tools in one corner. Inside the house, there were no animal bowls or cages, no pets at all, not even a goldfish. There were very few photos, which made the one prominently displayed on the mantel stand out: it showed a teenage girl and a middle-aged man.

Shevaun examined the picture of father and daughter standing, arms linked, in front of the Boston Opera House. She wondered idly what was so important about the event that it alone had been immortalized and framed. She also wondered where the mother of this family was. She knew that it was not utterly unusual for a man to raise a child alone in this day and age, but there was usually a story behind it.

The girl's bedroom was a horror, but only because of her taste in art. Picasso. Dalí. Shevaun shuddered. They might be considered geniuses, but Shevaun had been among the first to view Michelangelo's work on the Sistine Chapel. She had touched the *Mona Lisa.* She had fallen in love with *David*'s beauty. Shevaun might have learned to use modern inventions like computers and automobiles, but she refused to develop an appreciation for modern art. At least Rodin was an artist, even if it was tacky to have his work in wax on a student's cluttered desk instead of appropriately displayed.

Not cluttered, Shevaun realized as she studied Erin's desk more closely. It was almost fanatically neat, just like the rest of the room.

Where were the posters of bands and actors, the strewn clothing, the photos of friends taped to the mirror—all the things one expected in a teenage girl's room? Why Rodin, instead of some teen magazine? Why a rose window, instead of hearts and flowers?

Whether the girl was mad remained to be seen, but she wasn't quite average. People were drawn to art that reflected their own souls, their lusts and needs and fears. Picasso, Dalí, O'Keeffe, all the art Erin had chosen involved fractured images, perception twisted and shattered.

There was only one object in the room that was out of place. Twisted up with the blankets, half under a pillow, was a photo album. It quickly became clear why there were so few photographs in the house: someone objected to them.

Shevaun flipped through the album at random, without focusing on any individual image. Many of the pictures had been crumpled, or torn up and lovingly pieced together, taped and laminated onto the page. A large number of the pictures seemed to involve other kids with vacant expressions, standing or sitting in sterile locations, on chairs or industrial-style couches.

Nearer to the end of the album, there were quite a few images of a familiar young man. Though several years younger and a good deal more disheveled in these photos, the boy she had fed on at the café—a hyena shapeshifter, judging by his taste—was still recognizable by his vivid blue eyes and mischievous expression.

Shevaun smiled, recalling that smirk, only to frown as she realized *she* had never seen him look that way.

In one photograph, he was curled up, asleep, with a purple stuffed animal in his arms. In another, he was standing on a table in a dramatic pose, wearing a sheet like a costume toga. There was one image of him with his arm across the shoulders of a girl with short, wild brown hair; that picture had once been shredded.

Curious, Shevaun started working backward through the album. The photographs of strangers were intact, but every image involving the girl—almost certainly Erin—had been savaged.

Shevaun could picture the scene:

Waking and finding these cherished possessions destroyed. Weeping as she struggled to fit the pieces together with shaking hands. Ruining one photo with tears before a nurse tried to take them away . . . to throw them out—no, she couldn't—

Shevaun flung the album away and crossed her arms over her chest, shivering.

Almost against her will, her eyes dropped once more to the vile object, which had fallen open to the first page. There was just one picture, of a smiling woman with her arm linked around what seemed to be the man from the opera house photograph downstairs. The details were barely visible, as the photo had once been torn into tiny pieces—shredded by a determined, meticulous hand.

It's all I have—

Shevaun kicked the album closed, refusing to look more closely at that picture.

What had just happened? She had been there, inside a memory that wasn't hers. She could taste Erin's tears, feel her fury and pain—

God, it hurt, that pain. Pain and fear and anger like Shevaun hadn't known since . . . since the war, that last battle, when everything she had ever believed in had suddenly collapsed. She pressed a hand to her chest, half expecting to feel her heart pounding.

No!

Shevaun had given her life to rid herself of such feelings. She had run to the demon who had offered her immortality, and begged him to free her—

"Shevaun?"

Adjila was in the doorway. She flung herself into his arms, reminding herself who and where and when she was.

"I've got to kill her," she gasped. She couldn't seem to get enough air. . . . She was suffocating. "Now. She—where would she be now?"

"Shevaun—"

"School. It's Wednesday, right?" Why couldn't she breathe?

Adjila sighed, then hooked an arm around her throat, choking her, his feet braced against her struggles. What— why was Adjila *attacking* her?

He wasn't attacking her; he was reminding her that she hadn't needed to breathe in more than five hundred years.

As soon as she stopped fighting him, Adjila released her. "Feel better?" he asked.

"What just happened?"

"At a guess?" Adjila offered. "You were channeling her, though less completely than in Sète." He knelt beside the album Shevaun had thrown away. "This triggered it?"

She nodded, and Adjila tucked the book under his arm. "Erin Misrahe *is* at school. However, I don't think it would be wise to kill her until we understand exactly what she has done. Linked as you two are, her death could harm you."

Reluctantly, Shevaun nodded. She had no interest in the subtle working of power, in auras and magic. That was Adjila's area of expertise, so she trusted his warnings.

Realizing how early it still was, Shevaun asked with surprise, "Did you see Pandora already?" Adjila rarely visited the woman who had taught him to use his power and had made him immortal, and when he did, the visits tended to run long.

"She was working. I've been ordered to present myself tomorrow morning," Adjila said, with a smirk that revealed exactly how he felt about such a command. "We'll see what we can find out about the girl tonight. If it turns out we want Pandora's help, we should probably consider showing up."

"Then let's go find our human 'friend,'" Shevaun said, impatient.

"Let's get some rest first. You have to be as exhausted as I am. We can go find her after some sleep."

Sleep. Shevaun knew he was probably right, but sleep wouldn't offer the same instant gratification as the sound of a snapping neck, and Shevaun had never been very good at waiting.

Chapter 8

Erin fiddled with a pencil, working diligently on a sketch in an effort not to meet Tina's gaze.

"I know the name Adjila," Tina said. "Shevaun has never cooperatively discussed him with anyone, but she often asks where he is or demands his presence."

"When I woke up—well, thought I woke up—in that other place yesterday, I felt like maybe I had been leading a double life, that these other people really existed and had been as frightened by Shevaun's disappearance as my father would be by mine."

Erin spoke the words quietly as she drew another line. She had started drawing when she'd gone into therapy at eight years old, and had graduated from crayons to pencils quickly. It always made her feel better, and often helped her organize her memories during sessions. She had already done a quick sketch of the rooms from her dream, as well as she could remember them—which was quite vividly. She had not yet had the courage to try to draw Shevaun, the way she had looked in the mirror.

"Shevaun is deeply protective of Adjila," Tina said. "A dream like this could just be your mind's way of dealing with needing to let go of someone with whom part of you is, frankly, in love. It might have been triggered by the stress from recent changes, or just by the recognition of new attachments in your life. You said you're making new friends at fencing, didn't you?"

Erin nodded, smudging the graphite to soften a line before adding a highlight with the eraser. "Was making friends," she said, somewhat bitterly. "I think I've changed my mind about fencing."

They had already discussed Erin's aggressive thoughts during her fencing bout. Tina had suggested that they could have been perfectly normal competitive impulses, and had pointed out that Erin hadn't become violent or dissociated and had been firmly in her own mind when the coach had separated them.

Erin was less sure. She didn't want to risk another hallucination and panic attack. It would be safer just to slow down until she felt more in control again.

Tina's gaze flickered to the sketch, and she asked, "Is that him?"

Erin hadn't been paying attention to *what* she was drawing, focusing only on the individual shapes, lights, and shadows as she talked and listened to Tina, but now the face staring back at her from the page startled her.

Adjila.

Pencil alone did not do him justice. Oils—those were what she needed. Oils and a canvas—

She shoved the sketch away, crumpling it in her haste. She didn't paint, didn't know how to paint. For an instant, though, it had seemed like such a natural thought. Of course oils. They would be able to capture the depth of his gaze, which the flat graphite couldn't. They would be able to reveal the glow of his tanned skin and the strength of his limbs.

"Deep breath, Erin," Tina said.

Erin closed her eyes, following Tina's advice until she was steadier. She felt Tina take the picture from her hands.

"I don't think I want to talk about him right now," Erin said, feeling shaky.

"Okay," Tina replied. They had had a long client-therapist relationship, and Tina knew the difference between "I don't want to talk about it but I need to" and "I don't want to talk about it because I think it will trigger a panic attack and an episode." This was one of the latter. Tina said, "What about that printout you brought in with you? You said you wanted to talk about it before you left."

Oh, *that*. Hallucinations, dreams, and artwork aside, the e-mail Erin had received that morning had been as surprising as anything else could be. She handed it to Tina, who looked over the words Erin had already read a dozen times.

Erin,

It feels weird to be writing to you for the first time now. Three years, right? Well, you know how it goes. I heard from a friend of a friend of a shrink of a friend that you were a free bird now and back in Massachusetts. Anyway, I was at work and just couldn't quit thinking about you. I've got a slum of an apartment in Boston barely big enough to turn around in, but it's mine and if you're around, I'll give you a tour. Or maybe take you about the city, or just out to dinner? It could be fun to hang again, like old times minus the padded walls. I don't have a computer, so I don't check my e-mail unless I have time at work, but if you want a blast from the past, CALL ME. 6175552055.

—Sassy

PS Sorry I never wrote you until now. Had a lot of life to get together. You know how that is. If now's a bad time for you, I get that too. Hope to hear from you.

"Sassy?" Tina asked.

"Sherwood," Erin said, wincing. Sherwood James Kash hated his real name. No one but his parents and his doctors called him by it.

"Do you plan to call him?" Tina asked. The e-mail had been sent at a little past five that morning, too recently for Erin to have replied yet.

"I don't know." Erin took the printout and put it into her backpack. "Do you think I should?" Tina smiled a little, with an expression Erin recognized. Erin instantly rephrased her question. "I mean, do you think it would be a bad idea?"

"Why do *you* think it might be?"

"It's not like I was in good shape when we met," Erin said. "He's seen me in some less than brilliant moments." She self-consciously touched her hair. She had known Sassy for about two minutes before Shevaun had managed to get her hands on a plastic knife and, in a fit, sawed off Erin's waist-length hair. She hadn't grown it out past her chin since.

"And you've seen him in some equally 'brilliant' moments," Tina said. "Are you worried about the memories it might bring up, from the hospital?"

Erin shook her head. "The ward was the last full-time hospital I was in. They're the ones who finally got my medications working. And Sassy was . . ." She blushed as Tina quirked an eyebrow. ". . . a good friend," she finished defiantly.

She had had her first kiss with Sassy, when she was thirteen and he was fifteen years old. The orderlies hadn't known if they should separate them or be thrilled to see them engaging in healthy adolescent behavior. Erin had no idea how many details had made it into her records.

"If you want to call him, I don't see that it would hurt anything," Tina said.

"You said the dream might be a result of new attachments," Erin said. "Couldn't getting back in touch with him make them worse?"

"Any kind of change in your real life has the potential to affect your alter," Tina admitted, "but dreams can't hurt you. They may even be a very good sign. I can't promise that nothing new will trigger old and potentially unsettling memories, but I do believe you're strong enough to work through those memories."

The session ended with Erin not feeling much better. She tried to put on a brave face, however, and pay attention in her other classes before her father dropped her off at the public school that afternoon. She was a couple of minutes early, so she wandered into the cafeteria, wondering if she would be able to find Marissa.

Would Marissa even be in school that day? She had just lost two family members. Erin couldn't even imagine how Marissa must be feeling. It seemed so different from Erin's loss, when she was too young to feel the pain of her mother's death. One of her greatest terrors growing up had been that she might, while dissociating, hurt her father, and lose him, too.

Even contemplating losing him pushed Erin to the brink of another panic attack, so she pushed the thoughts away, trying to focus on something productive.

She sat near the edge of the cafeteria and scrolled through the few numbers on her cell phone. Marissa was in there. Should Erin call to see how she was doing? No, she should wait to see if Marissa was in class first.

Once the phone was in her hand and the contacts list

was open, however, she found herself looking at the name after Marissa's: *Sassy*. She had programmed in the number from his e-mail that morning.

If nothing else, she wouldn't have to worry about explaining anything to him. Sassy knew exactly who and what she was. He knew the things she was afraid of, and unlike Marissa, he understood that she had a reason to be afraid. He had seen what she was capable of.

That was also partly why she hadn't spoken to him in three years. She had needed time to decide who *else* she was, beyond the bounds of places like the ward.

Erin dialed and held her breath while the phone rang. Maybe it was a good idea, and maybe it wasn't, but Sassy had made the effort to get in touch and she found that she wanted to reply.

It was halfway through the fourth ring before someone answered. "Mmhuh?" He sounded like she had woken him up.

"Sassy?"

"Erin?" he responded, grogginess replaced by bright enthusiasm.

"Hi."

What to say next escaped her, but luckily Sassy had never in his life been at a loss for words. "I'm glad you called. I'm sure my e-mail must have seemed really out of the blue."

His voice sounded exactly the way it always had, smooth and *trustworthy*, even when he was lying through his teeth.

It reminded her of his ability to fast-talk nurses and therapists into almost anything. "Pretty much, yeah."

"I've thought about you a lot the last couple years, but, well, it never seemed like a good time."

"A couple of months ago it wouldn't have been," she admitted, thinking about how the conversation might have gone if he had e-mailed her in June, when she was still fighting with her father and doctors about going to "real" school. "But—"

"Who're you talking to?" Erin hadn't been looking around, and was startled when Marissa suddenly sat beside her.

"But?" Sassy prompted. "May I take that to mean *this* month you would be open to getting together?"

"Yeah, I—" Marissa leaned closer, and Erin shifted the phone to her opposite ear. "I would be."

"Do you want to meet somewhere, or—wait, you probably don't drive yet."

"I don't think my therapist would trust me with a car even if I was old enough," she said.

"I'll pick you up, then, and we can stay somewhere local," he offered. "It'll keep your father from coming after me with a shotgun."

She had almost forgotten that he was two years older than she was. It hadn't mattered much before. "That'd be good." She kept her reply simple, since Marissa was still blatantly eavesdropping.

"Dinner?" Sassy suggested.

"Dinner?" Marissa echoed, making Erin wish she had thought to turn down the volume on her phone.

"We have an audience," Erin informed him. "And yes, dinner would be great."

"Ah, you know I love an audience," Sassy quipped.

"Have you changed *at all* in the last three years?" she asked, laughing.

"I'm a bona fide productive member of society now. You'll see. So, dinner. Tonight?"

Tonight? That was a little soon. "It's a school night."

Marissa snatched the phone and said, "Tonight is perfect. Can you pick her up from school?"

"Marissa!" Erin hissed as she took back the phone. "Sorry. That's a friend of mine."

"No problem," Sassy said. "Which school and what time?"

"Nefershen Public," Erin answered.

"You're at the public school now?" Sassy asked. "Congratulations. Seriously, that's exciting. I know how much you always wanted to go."

"Thanks. But maybe we—"

"Bring him by fencing," Marissa said.

"Fencing?" Sassy asked. "They let you handle a sword these days?"

"I'm not staying on the team," she said with a sigh. Marissa looked like she was about to say something, but bit her lip and shook her head. "Maybe we should do something later instead, so I'll have a chance to go home and get ready and stuff."

"Nuh-uh," Marissa said, shaking her head to veto that idea. She grabbed the phone again. "Three o'clock is great," she said to Sassy. "Come by the gym." She handed the phone back to Erin with a sweet smile and said, "I don't know what life was like for you before, but in the real world, you do not get to go out with a boy without your girlfriends meeting him."

"I'm not even allowed to . . . I don't know, primp first?" Erin protested, though honestly, she had just wanted the extra time to keep her two lives from intersecting just yet.

"The first time I kissed you," Sassy recalled, "you had just cut your hair off with a plastic knife. You were in restraints, and your lips were completely chapped and dry from the tranquilizers. The next day, you tried to kill me with a torn-off piece of bedsheet. I've seen you at your worst. You hardly need to dress up for me."

Marissa whistled as Erin blushed.

"I—okay," Erin stammered. "But wait—I still have to ask my dad if he's even okay with this." She didn't think he would be thrilled about her taking off for dinner with a boy in the middle of the week after having had a panic attack the day before.

"I'll call him," Sassy replied with an audible grin. "He likes me."

That was probably one of Sassy's more grandiose lies, since Erin didn't think there was a father alive who *liked* the first boy caught making out with his daughter. However, she had all the faith in the world that Sassy's fast talking *would* get her father to agree to let her go out for a little while.

"Then I'll see you at three."

"See you then."

Erin hung up, feeling dazed. It wasn't like Marissa had never been pushy before, but Erin wasn't sure why she felt the need to be so assertive about meeting Sassy. Maybe it was one of the parts of socialization that had flown past her due to her never having had this kind of friendship before, which meant that maybe she should be happy about it.

She could be grateful later. For now, she just hoped she wouldn't regret it.

Chapter 9

"YOU'RE STILL GOING TO FENCING?" Erin asked as they walked toward the gym after a halfhearted session of mutual tutoring. Erin had been too nervous to concentrate, and Marissa had been understandably withdrawn between bursts of what was obviously forced cheer.

"Of course," she answered. "I'm fine, Erin. Or, no, I'm not fine, but I'll *be* fine. This is how I deal. I have to keep moving and doing the things I have to do. Some quality violence this afternoon will help," she added, with a feral grin that reminded Erin unnervingly of her hallucination of the tiger.

"Is there going to be a service?" Erin asked, hoping Marissa would have a time when she would let herself feel her own pain, surrounded by family.

Marissa shook her head. "My culture," she said haltingly, "doesn't really do funerals. And I'm kind of estranged from the rest of the family. It's complicated."

Erin was horrified by the depth of her own ignorance. Marissa had never spoken about her family or her background before, so Erin had just assumed that everything was normal. As if Erin had any right to make assumptions about what "normal" meant. "Marissa, if you need—"

"You're a good friend, Erin," Marissa interrupted, "and I wish I could explain, but I've got to get through this in my own way, okay?"

Erin forced herself to nod. Marissa had referred earlier to some kind of group that would help her through it, so at least she wasn't trying to cope completely on her own. Erin wished she could help, but she couldn't do anything unless Marissa wanted her to.

"Besides," Marissa said, "I *do* want to meet this boyfriend of yours. I'm excited for you."

"He's not my boyfriend," Erin said, accepting the change of topic. "I haven't seen him in three years. He just e-mailed me with no warning."

"And you answered him," Marissa said, "which means he means *something* to you. You blushed at least twice while on the phone with him, which makes me think he's more than just a friend. So why are you so skittish about seeing him?"

Erin *was* excited about seeing Sassy, but this was all so sudden. Her last memory of him was their hastily exchanging e-mail addresses as his parents talked to the psychologists and signed the paperwork for his release. They had written a couple of times while she had still been in the ward, but somehow they had lost touch. She wasn't even sure which one of them had sent the last e-mail, but it had been years ago.

"I'm just nervous," she said to Marissa. With a half smile, she admitted, "I tend to be nervous about a lot of things, you may have noticed."

"It'll be fine," Marissa assured her. "And fun. Oh, it's almost three!" she said, glancing down at her watch. "I need to check the gym and make sure none of the frosh are getting into trouble before the coach arrives. Don't dare leave before I get back!"

Erin brushed her hair and tossed a mint into her mouth. Not that this was a date, but she could still make an effort to look nice, right? As she was putting her brush back into her bag, someone wrapped an arm around her waist, and before she could think, she had flipped him over her shoulder and he'd sprawled full-length on the floor.

"Holy . . . *ow*."

"Oh—god, *Sassy*. Sorry." She tumbled to her knees next to him.

"Erin? Everything's . . . so cold. . . . Kiss me, love, as everything goes dark. . . ."

She smacked his shoulder. "Oh, get up. If you can be melodramatic, you're fine."

His eyelashes fluttered as he opened his eyes a fraction. "I don't even get a pity kiss?" He opened his eyes completely and grinned. "Oh, well. I should've known better than to startle you, anyway." He looked past her and called out, "It's all right. I'm a professional stuntman. I do things like this all the time."

"Stuntman, huh?" Erin asked as she offered him a hand and pulled him to his feet. He moved stiffly but didn't complain about the rough reception.

"More or less." He shrugged. "Introduce me to our charming audience?"

She turned around, bracing herself for Marissa's good-natured teasing. "This is—" She hesitated when she realized that Marissa's eyes were wide with surprise. It could have had something to do with Erin's flipping her "date" onto the floor, but Marissa and Sassy had locked gazes with something akin to hostility. "Marissa?"

Marissa took a deep breath, and the surprise on her face shifted to confusion. "And this must be Sassy," she said.

Sassy recovered, his expression going through a mercurial change until even his eyes, seemed to smile. "Indeed I am," he said. "Well, more rightly I am Samuel Eben Mergentry the third, though I go by Sassy so as not to be confused with my father and his father. My father, Samuel Eben Mergentry the second, was a marine, and my mother was the third wife of a Pakistani sheik before she and my father ran off together and were married in the Americas. I hope that's a suitable pedigree for you."

To those who didn't know that the words were complete bull, they would be nearly believable. Sassy was tall, and broader in the shoulders than Erin remembered, but with the same dusky complexion, courtesy of—so *she* had been told—his Israeli father. The rich tone of his skin and his black hair, now long enough that he had it pulled back in a rubber band, made his blue eyes all the more striking.

"And you work as a stunt double?" Marissa asked, obviously skeptical.

"It distressed my father terribly when, after all his training, I sold my soul to Hollywood instead of the army."

"We're going to leave now," Erin announced, catching Sassy's arm to guide him away.

"Wait," Marissa said. This time, the teasing lilt to her voice sounded forced. "Erin doesn't get to walk away with tall-dark-and-handsome without my knowing more."

"Tall, dark, *and* handsome, eh?" Sassy echoed. "That's my mother's side, of course. My father was an ugly, short little fellow."

"So, you two met . . ." Marissa trailed off, waiting for Sassy and Erin to fill in the rest.

Sassy looked at Erin, leaving the answer up to her, which meant he didn't mind if she told the truth.

"We were in the same psych ward for about six months," Erin said. She didn't have Sassy's suavity, but then, the truth was never as exciting as the stories he could tell.

"Well, then." Marissa hesitated. "I imagine it's rude to ask what for."

"Nymphomania, and persecution complex due to my extreme wealth," Sassy answered good-naturedly. "It is a great loss to the world that I have now been cured of both."

Marissa sighed, then asked bluntly, "He's the one who took the last seat in the compulsive liar class, isn't he?"

"And why they let me out, we may never know," Sassy

murmured. "Anyway, unless you have other questions—which I would be delighted to answer, I assure you—Erin and I should get on with our nefarious plans." Marissa hesitated, and Sassy chuckled. "Erin, I do believe your overzealous friend is trying to protect *you* from *me*. Would you please remind her that you are more than capable of defending yourself, and I have the new bruises on my back to prove it?"

"You startled me," Erin said apologetically.

"That was stupid of me," he admitted. "I'd forgotten what your reflexes are like when you aren't sedated. So, do you still like Greek food?"

Erin grinned as Marissa looked puzzled by the sudden shift in topic. Spending time with Sassy was a little like getting caught in a riptide. "I love Greek. How on Earth do you remember things like that?"

"Look," Marissa said, touching Sassy's arm, "I work with SingleEarth. I—"

Sassy cut Marissa off with a look so sharp *Erin* flinched. It was hard to remember his ever being so cold with anyone. Had he changed, or had she just never noticed?

His voice, however, was still light when he said, "I'm not a fan. You're a friend of Erin's and that's great, I suppose, but you and yours can keep away from me, thank you very much." With that, he held out his arm to Erin like an old-fashioned gentleman. "Shall we?"

Erin hesitated, glancing back at Marissa, who just shrugged. Erin had no idea what the interlude between her two friends had been about.

"I'll explain later, or she will," Sassy said, as if reading her thoughts. "It's kind of complicated. Can we eat first?"

Sassy had often been moody—mostly in the presence of authority—but Erin trusted him never to hurt her.

Nodding, Erin took his arm. "Let's go."

Chapter 10

DESPITE THE STRANGE ENCOUNTER with Marissa, Erin couldn't help being entertained by Sassy's rapid chatter. By the time their appetizer arrived, her sides hurt from laughing. The last thing she wanted to do was ask Sassy what had obviously upset him earlier.

"Of course you would get the appetizer they light on *fire*," Erin joked as their dish was delivered to the table.

"The pyromania was never officially diagnosed," Sassy said, extinguishing the saganaki and serving them both. "Cheese and fire: how can you get any better? Speaking of, how's your dad been?

"*Speaking of?* How did you get from cheese to my dad?"

"No idea; that's the schizophrenia."

"I'm the schizophrenic. You're the compulsive . . . well, everything, as far as I could tell. And my dad is doing great, though he sounded a little nervous when he called to ask if I really planned to go out with you today. My curfew is seven, by the way, after which I'm pretty sure he'll send wild dogs after you."

"It was the craziest thing," Sassy said. "I was at work—did I tell you I actually have a job? I sell coffee to surly college students."

"They let you handle money? That's new."

"Cash was never exciting. It's all the wires that are hard to resist—it's an Internet café," he added by way of explanation. "Anyway, I was working the night shift, and suddenly . . ." He paused and tilted his head. "Well, that's just the weirdest thing."

"Hmm?"

"I had completely forgotten about the girl. She came in near the end of my shift." He shook his head as if to clear it. "She's what made me start thinking about you, I think. Not that you two look anything alike; it's more that—" He frowned.

"You start telling a story, you can't stop there," Erin said when it became obvious that he was lost in thought and not about to continue.

"She didn't remind me of *you*," he said carefully, "so much as she reminded me of Shevaun." A shiver ran down Erin's spine. "Sorry."

"It's all right. A little weird, but all right. If she didn't *look* like me, how could she remind you of . . . you know?"

"Shevaun *doesn't* look like you," he said. "In her head, anyway. She carries herself differently than you do. She speaks

89

differently, and has a different accent. She has little mannerisms I started to watch out for, since you picked them up when you were about to shift over."

"Such as?"

"Such as . . . well, the way she tosses her head, as if to get long hair off her face, or the stance she takes when she's expecting a fight." He paused to think. "She has light hands, and touches things delicately, even when she's using them as weapons. And she has this way of going still while she evaluates a situation."

"I never realized you knew her that well." They had never talked about Shevaun before, since her name alone had once had the power to trigger panic attacks or full-out psychotic episodes.

Sassy picked at his food. "She was part of you, so I wasn't about to hate her. And she was a part of you that sometimes tried to *kill* me, so she was worth watching out for." He paused to search Erin's face, as if checking to make sure the conversation wasn't distressing her, before he continued. "I talked to her once or twice. Sometimes if you were really tired, or seriously tranquilized, you'd switch over without her even noticing where she was."

"What kinds of things would she say?"

"Well, I used to be wicked jealous of this Adjila guy," he said with a bit of a smirk. "I couldn't understand everything, since despite my remarkable memory, I lack your savantlike language skills and she didn't tend to talk in English. Your hair really bothered her, but I guess you knew that." Erin understood why now: in her dream, the hair that had tumbled past Shevaun's shoulders had been beautiful, wavy, and auburn. Seeing Erin's own straight brown hair must have been torture for Shevaun. That would also explain her tendency to break mirrors and destroy photographs of Erin. "Sometimes you would ramble about your heartbeat, of all things."

"You never told me any of this."

"The first couple of times it happened, I called nurses over, but you got violent and had to be restrained. Eventually I decided it was best to just stay with you, make sure you didn't do anything you'd regret." He seemed to consider for a moment, then confided, "She kisses differently than you do."

"You *kissed* my alter?" Erin gasped. "My psychopathic, homicidal alter?"

"In my defense, it's not like I was in the ward because I was of sound mind."

"That's just creepy. Please tell me that's as far as it went."

"That's as far as it went."

"Are you lying?"

"Yes, but never mind it. Look, dinner's here. Perfect timing."

"Sassy—"

He grinned at her. "That's as far as it went. Honest. The fear she would wake up and bite my tongue off kept me in check."

They ate mostly in silence for a few minutes before Erin gathered the courage to say, "So. Are you going to tell me what that was about, with Marissa?"

Sassy drummed his fingers on the table once before asking, "Do I have to?"

"I can always ask her," Erin said, "if you would rather not talk about it."

"She'll lie to you." He chuckled, as if recognizing the irony of his own statement. "SingleEarth . . . is an organization that deals with the kind of stuff that put me in the ward in the first place." He looked up at Erin, who waited, knowing that further questions would just push him into an easy lie. "It's kind of a new age hospital. I found them about a year after the ward let me out. I had a lot of questions and they said they had answers, but it was all crap. When I was in pain and just wanted someone to fix me, they preached at me and talked about how I should want to be living. And when I wanted guidance and answers about *why,* all they gave me was population statistics and biomedical explanations. They have a lot of philosophies I disagree with, a lot of which fall along the lines of 'what you don't know can't hurt you.' Since what I didn't know nearly *killed* me, and made me and everyone around me miserable for several years, I kind of disagreed with their definition of 'need to know.' "

He shook his head and started pulling apart the last of his dinner, concentrating on that. Marissa had told Sassy that she worked with SingleEarth, but Erin wondered if it was also the group helping her through the deaths in her family. If she frequented a hospital like that, especially if she did it both as staff and patient, it would explain why she handled Erin's confession so well.

"Anyway," Sassy said, "maybe they're good for some people, and maybe they've been good to your friend Marissa, but you know how well I deal with people who treat me like an invalid child."

Yes, she did. She had never seen Sassy physically violent, but his words could do plenty of damage when he chose, most often to those who patronized him—or lied to him.

Erin changed the subject by talking about her annoying literature class; then Sassy lightened the mood with tales of his completely fictional exploits, and as dinner wrapped up, they stumbled out of the restaurant, chortling over one of their past escapades.

"But it was *purple*!" Erin gasped. "So . . . very . . . purple!"

"Yes, but you don't—you don't understand the—" Sassy gave up on his retort, which was quickly lost to laughter.

He held out his arm, which she took as if no time had passed, leaning on him as she struggled for breath.

They had finally both calmed down enough to walk upright when Sassy whispered under his breath, "Well, maybe kind of mauve," which started the hilarity up again.

It didn't quiet until they were both standing beside Sassy's car, eyes sparkling from memories of their strange mutual past. Erin managed to say, "You know, that's one of those stories I don't think I would ever be able to explain to *anyone*."

"No, you *really* had to be there," Sassy said. "I thought I was losing my mind . . . um, more."

"No, it really was that"—snicker—"*purple*. Poor nurse."

"Good times," Sassy breathed. "Good times indeed."

"You know, I never knew what you were in for. You must have told me a score of contradictory things. I know about some of the compulsive stuff, because I saw it for myself, but I never . . ." She shrugged.

"You mean, what actually got me committed?"

"Yeah."

The ward wasn't a place people went unless they were considered dangerous to themselves or others, or otherwise so far gone nowhere else felt capable of handling them.

"You don't have to say, if you don't want to."

Sassy paused, considered, and then put his keys back into his pocket and leaned against the car to tell his story.

"Most of it had been going on for a while, without my parents knowing about it. I could fake my dad's voice and his signature, so they didn't hear about the detentions and suspensions—fights at school, telling teachers where to shove it, setting an exam on fire, stuff like that." Erin forced a smile to match Sassy's expression, which looked as strained as hers felt. "I know I've given you a lot of weird stories about my parents, but really, they're . . . pretty cool. I tried not to hurt them. They only realized that I was in trouble when the police brought me home for the first time, after I had been caught walking out of a computer store with something expensive enough for them to call the cops. Naturally, I responded real well to the men in blue. I'm lucky I was fourteen, and a scrawny fourteen at that, so I got some 'pity.' The judge—who also learned about my actions at school—recommended a full psychological evaluation."

"And that's when you ended up in the ward?"

He shook his head. "Nah, that's when I ended up in a private school for troubled teens. I was there for maybe half a year, until I walked into class one day with both wrists slit, having taken a whole bottle of my mother's prescription migraine medication. Needless to say, I didn't get far. I passed out, and one stomach pumping and some vascular surgery later, I woke up in the ward, where I languished for the next six months.

"And that, dear Erin," he said, concluding, "is probably more truth in a two-minute span than I've told anyone in the last year."

Finally, she asked the one question she had always wanted to know the answer to: "Why?"

"Why tell you the truth?"

She shook her head. "No. Why . . . why the stealing, the lying . . . everything. You said your parents were great. Did something *happen,* or—" Sassy's expression had closed off, so she stopped. "You don't have to tell me. I just always wondered. All my life I've wanted to be normal. I never got why people would do things like that by choice."

Sassy let out a long, slow breath. "I guess I didn't feel like I had a choice. You know how it is, when reality is one way to you, but different to everyone else. You want to tell them, but they would call you crazy, so you learn to say what they want to hear. Eventually there isn't a right answer, just the lies and the anger."

"What was the truth?"

A long silence fell after she asked the question. Finally, Sassy shook his head.

"Maybe another time. Not tonight. Please."

"Okay." She leaned back against him. "Just so you know, I would never call you crazy. I've got you beat by a long shot. Just the other day I thought I saw my friend Marissa turn into a tiger."

His eyes widened. "Erin—"

She shrugged. "It's okay. It was a fluke, that's it. Though I had this wild dream after, where I woke up *as* Shevaun, in her house somewhere in France. My therapist is really hopeful it—" She broke off, because someone had just stepped into her line of sight down the block, someone familiar. "Sassy . . . do you see . . ."

Sassy looked up, following her gaze. "That guy?"

"He's really there?"

He nodded. "Yeah. Blond hair, kinda tan, light eyes— maybe blue? Hard to tell from here."

Erin took a deep breath and tried to stay calm. The man bore a perfect resemblance to someone who wasn't supposed to exist outside her imagination, and he was walking straight toward them.

"Do you know him?" Sassy asked.

"God, I hope not."

"Excuse me," the man said. His voice was so familiar it made her heart thump.

"Yes?" Sassy asked curtly.

Erin put a hand on Sassy's arm. "It's okay. Are you . . ." The man appeared mildly amused as he looked back and forth between her and Sassy. That too, the quietly smug amusement, felt familiar. "Do I know you?" she blurted out.

"Apparently," he replied, which made Sassy bristle more. "Erin, why don't you introduce me to the puppy before he starts growling?"

Erin expected Sassy to respond strongly to the insulting though bizarre term. Instead, he paled.

"Look," she snapped, reacting to Sassy's odd unease, "I'm sorry, but I don't have the faintest idea *who* you are or *what* you want—"

"Don't you?" the stranger asked. "Let's try an experiment."

Fed up, Erin said, "Come on, Sassy. Let's get out of—"

He cut her off, invading her space, stepping so close that she should have pulled away, *would* have pulled away if only his eyes hadn't been locked on hers. She had stared deeply into those eyes many times.

All thoughts ground to a halt as he caressed her cheek and wrapped a hand around the back of her neck. As he kissed her, Erin closed her eyes with a sigh.

Chapter 11

ADJILA IGNORED FOR THE MOMENT the fact that he was kissing a sixteen-year-old human girl. This wasn't a matter of love or lust, but of scientific inquiry. Do this, and—

The boy Erin had called Sassy flung himself at them, sending Erin to the ground.

Or, to be more accurate, sending *Shevaun* to the ground. She twisted, pushing herself up with a familiar hiss as Adjila looped an arm around the boy's neck to control him.

Sassy had already gone still, not struggling anymore. "What did you do?"

"Exposed Erin to something more familiar to Shevaun's mind than her own," Adjila answered. Shevaun's reaction to Adjila's kiss supported Erin's claim that she hadn't formed this connection intentionally. Otherwise, Adjila would not have been able to trigger the switch so easily.

Shevaun's eyes widened as she looked at the boy. "The tasty shapeshifter from the coffee shop," she pronounced with a smile. "I seem to keep seeing you about."

As Shevaun paused, looking away from Sassy and frowning as if struggling to recall something, there was something about her expression that didn't seem quite right to Adjila. This wasn't Shevaun, even though she certainly wasn't Erin.

Of course, he knew that the *real* Shevaun was hunting in the city. She didn't even know he was here; if she had, she would have insisted on accompanying him, and that was likely to complicate things. Adjila wanted a chance to examine Erin, and the strange connection she had with Shevaun, before his partner did something rash.

Adjila released his captive. The boy backed up a couple of paces, but did not run even though Adjila could tell from his sheet-white face and trembling hands that he wanted to.

"Shevaun?" Adjila asked. He had known vampires and some other Triste witches who could control a human's thoughts and actions for a while, but it wasn't the kind of thing that happened accidentally. He didn't know what other power could have caused what could only be accurately described as possession.

"I'm getting sick of this," the girl replied with Shevaun's tone and expression.

"Shevaun," Sassy squeaked.

"Yes," she snarled. "And you—"

She broke off in midsentence and studied her hand, which she had scraped when she'd fallen. If Shevaun had been in her real body, it would have healed instantly, but this wasn't her hand—it was Erin's—and she had finally noticed that. She reached up, feeling her short, straight hair and breathing quickly enough that Adjila feared she would faint if she didn't get her emotions in check. It had been a long time since Shevaun had been mortal.

"Calm down," Sassy said. "Take a deep breath. You'll hurt—yourself."

Her, the boy had almost said. Of all of them, Sassy seemed to be the least surprised by this transformation. That was almost as curious as the fact that Shevaun remembered meeting him. Adjila doubted it was a coincidence that Shevaun had been drawn to someone Erin was obviously close to.

Adjila moved forward and put a hand on Shevaun's forehead. One gentle push of power later, her heartbeat had calmed; he forced the panic away. He expected her to object to his using his magic to manipulate her fierce, fluctuating emotions, but she just bit her lip and looked at him with trusting eyes.

Again, the reaction was wrong. This woman lacked much of Shevaun's fire and instead seemed steeped with uncertainty.

"What's the last thing you remember?" he asked her.

"Going to sleep with you this morning."

"That's what you always remember last," Sassy said quietly. "Going to sleep."

Well, that was interesting.

"Is this the girl?" Shevaun asked.

Adjila nodded.

"I thought . . . How did I . . ."

Sassy had cautiously moved a little closer. "You remember Erin?" he asked.

"Of course I *remember* that—"

"Not 'of course,' " Sassy interrupted. "You've never remembered her before, never known she even *existed* before."

"Before?" Adjila asked.

He could see the boy trying to decide whether he should answer and how much he should say. He had conquered his panic swiftly, and Adjila could almost hear the rapid calculations going through his mind. Apparently, he had already accepted that Shevaun really did exist and wasn't simply a creation of a madwoman. Most mortals, even those with powerful blood such as a shapeshifter's, did not adjust their views of reality so easily.

A glance at the boy's mind explained part of that ability. His thoughts were slick and rapid, meshing together and then breaking apart in an odd pattern that made them hard to read. At another time, Adjila would have enjoyed analyzing why and how the boy had learned to do this and what it served to accomplish. For now, though, he had larger matters on his mind.

"Episodes like this have been happening to Erin most of her life," Sassy explained. "Does your Shevaun ever remember?"

"What do you mean, *his*?" Shevaun growled, obviously annoyed that they were talking around her. Adjila never would have done so if she had been the real Shevaun, but it was hard to take her seriously when she was poised in the body of a mortal child.

Sassy, however, jumped at the venom in Shevaun's voice, and this time he chose to speak directly to her instead of to Adjila. "Erin has been hospitalized most of her life, because every now and then, she wakes up as you. Every time it happens, you behave as if it has never happened before. This is the first time you've had any knowledge of her."

"I have to wonder, if you care about this girl, why you let her think she was crazy all her life," Adjila said.

"*I thought she was!*" The shapeshifter spun away, rubbing a hand over the back of his neck. "What was I supposed to think? I barely even knew what *I* was when I met her in the hospital. I figured she was just what they said—schizophrenic and dissociative. I wasn't going to rock her world by telling her about things that go bump in the night just for the hell of it. What have you done to her?"

"Us?" Shevaun said. "To *her*? Your girlfriend is the one who started this, who—"

"Does Erin remember being in Shevaun's body?" Adjila asked. The girl beside him might have Shevaun's memories—*most* of them, at least—but if the boy was correct, then once this episode was over, this ghost would simply be gone. She was an incomplete copy. That meant there wasn't much use in explaining things to her.

The boy nodded. "Only once that I know of. Recently, in fact, when Erin was sleeping. She thinks it was a dream."

"It only happened once," Shevaun growled.

Though Adjila still had no theories about how the connection between the girl and the vampire had been formed, the timing of Erin's appearance in Shevaun's world made sense. The way Adjila had subdued Shevaun's power to heal her after the hunters' attack must have left her vulnerable and allowed Erin's consciousness to intrude on Shevaun's.

"I think we should experiment," Shevaun suggested suddenly.

Adjila nodded distractedly. He was already using much of his attention to try to read Erin's aura. The task was made difficult by the profusion of drugs she had in her system. They seemed to be suppressing any power she might possess.

Shevaun leaned against him and whispered, "Really. I think we need to. We should see what this body is capable of, and what it responds to. After all, you *did* wake me with a kiss, didn't you?"

"Absolutely not!" The vehement protest, naturally, came from Sassy, before Adjila could even move to set the girl away. Even if Erin had Shevaun's memories, her body was practically that of a child. Adjila had no intention of taking this any further than his kiss.

Sassy launched himself at them again, but this time Adjila batted the irritating shapeshifter aside while he kept Shevaun at arm's length.

"Please. Don't do this to Erin," the boy said.

"Why not?" Shevaun asked. "She tried to kill Adjila with my body. I might as well have some fun with hers. Hmm. When I'm through with her, how do you think your Erin would like to wake up surrounded by bodies, holding a weapon with her own fingerprints on it?"

Sassy sounded like he was gritting his teeth as he said, "I can't believe I'm going to say anything that could help you, but . . ." He drew a deep, shaking breath. "Erin is on a lot of medication. She has to take it in the morning and evening. Even if she hadn't already missed a dose, putting her body through any significant . . . exertion . . . will almost definitely make her throw up, and might give her a heart attack."

Shevaun frowned, clearly less interested in the drawbacks of mortality than she was in her original plans to play.

"She carries her medication with her," Sassy said, sounding beaten.

Adjila was almost certain there was more going on in the boy's mind than he was letting on. If so, it was impressive; not many people could lie with their aura the way they lied with their tone. "It should keep her . . . I mean, them . . . safe. I know I can't stop you from doing whatever you are determined to do, but I don't think you want to kill Erin. Please. Just don't hurt her."

Adjila suspected some kind of trap, but he wanted to be rid of this doll, so he just shrugged.

"Fine," Shevaun said. "Where is this alchemy?"

Chapter 12

ONCE AGAIN, ERIN FOUND HERSELF awake in darkness. Squinting, she could barely bring into focus a single shaft of light falling beneath a curtain across the room, and she couldn't roll over. Her hands were tied together and attached to the headboard, and someone was spooned against her back.

She didn't feel injured, though her body was heavy and sore and her mouth was cottony. She closed her eyes again, trying to remember how she got here and, for that matter, where and when "here" was. She had gone to dinner with Sassy on Wednesday night. They had been by the car. . . . That man.

Adjila. Oh, god, was she with *him*?

She couldn't stop the small panicked sound that came from her throat at that moment and woke her bedmate.

"Erin?"

"*Sassy?*" The name came out in a relieved rush of breath. "What happened?"

Instead of answering, he leaned over, tilted her head back, and kissed her.

"Hi to you, too," she replied when he pulled back. "But I'm not liking the tied-up thing."

"Just checking," he said as he reached to release her wrists.

She kisses differently than you do, he had said. Well, that was one way to figure out who she was. That he needed to check was what had her concerned.

"Where are we?"

"My apartment," he answered. "I didn't want to take you home, because I was worried you might end up back in the hospital."

"Sassy, my dad is going to call the freaking *police*—"

"Yeah. He nearly did. I called him, told him you had a panic attack and took some pills and were sleeping on my floor for the night. Then I promised you would call in the morning, and tried to sound puzzled when he said things like 'drive her home this instant.' You might want to call him now, before the police *do* show up."

"Where's my phone?" She stumbled out of bed, rolling her shoulders, which were sore from the position in which they had been tied. Sassy snapped on the light, making her squint and cover her eyes for a moment as he retrieved her cell phone from his kitchen counter.

"What *did* happen?" she asked as she dialed. "And did it

occur to you that maybe, given my record, it would have been *better* for me to wake up in a hospital?"

"You're not crazy."

"Bull— Hi, Daddy," she said as her father picked up the phone halfway through the first ring.

"Erin? Are you all right?" She smiled a little, because his voice held less of the fear she would expect if he had believed Sassy's story about the panic attack, and more of the fear that made sense in the voice of a father whose daughter had never come home from a date.

"I had a bit of an episode last night," she answered.

There was silence on the other end, perhaps as her father decided whether he wanted to believe that any more than he did his suspicions.

"Sassy took care of me. He was a perfect gentleman." As much as he ever was, at least. "Given the way I feel, I think I took a double dose of pills and passed out." She saw Sassy nod.

"Erin . . ." Her father paused.

"I'll get the whole story from Sassy, and then get a ride home," she assured him, knowing it was probably no assurance at all. "I'll see you soon, Dad."

"Wait, Erin—"

She winced as she ended the call. "Okay, Sass, please tell me there's a good reason I just hung up on my dad."

"You remember that guy?" Sassy asked. "Adjila?"

She nodded slowly. "I was kind of hoping that was a holdover from my switching."

"No, he actually exists," Sassy said. "He exists; he knows

that both Erin and Shevaun exist; and he triggered you. Intentionally."

She sat down hard on the side of the bed. "He's not supposed to exist."

"Worse, Shevaun now knows Erin exists, too."

"My therapist would say that's a good thing," Erin said, though the words felt hollow. "The personalities both recognizing each other."

"Yeah, well, maybe it's a good thing for a crazy person, but you aren't crazy."

"Don't start with that, Sassy. *Please.* Just tell me what happened after I switched over."

He leaned back against the wall of the dingy little room. "I drugged her."

"Excuse me?"

"Shevaun and Adjila were hoping to play. I didn't want your body doing anything you wouldn't want it to do, so I convinced her to take some of the tranquilizers you keep in your bag. Shevaun might know a half dozen languages, art, and biology, but she doesn't know much about modern psychopharmacology. The meds kicked in while they were still debating what to do. When Shevaun started to get woozy, Adjila realized what I had done, but Shevaun told him to back off and leave me alone. He didn't seem like he was going to go for it at first, but when she—well, *you*—passed out, he just walked off. There was some other conversation in there, but apparently you don't want to hear anything that doesn't fit in your crazy-schema."

The defensive glint in his eye was very familiar. Erin

had seen it many times when he'd faced therapists and orderlies.

She drew a deep breath, squaring off.

"How long a drive is it from here to my house?" she asked.

"Erin—"

"How long?"

"Maybe forty minutes," he said, sounding resigned. "There shouldn't be much traffic *leaving* the city at this hour."

"Then grab your keys. You have forty minutes to try to explain to me how, for the last sixteen years, I've been notcrazy. Because that's kind of a lot for me to just accept on a whim."

He nodded slowly and fished a set of keys off the nightstand.

"Sure. We'll talk in the car."

She followed him silently down two flights of stairs and outside, where his car was parallel parked across the street.

"Do you need directions to my house?" she asked, mostly for something to say, as they climbed into the car.

"I guess I should get those," Sassy answered.

"I'll ask my dad." Sassy didn't respond, focusing instead on squeezing his car free of its parking space. "I should let him know I'm on my way home, anyway."

Her father once again answered immediately. "Erin?"

"Hey. Sorry to hang up on you before," she said. "Sassy was being . . . Sassy," she said vaguely. "But we're on our way home now. Can you give Sassy directions?"

"You don't know how to get to your own house?" Sassy asked as Erin handed him the phone.

"You try learning your way around a town after spending eight years in hospital wards," she snapped. Even after two years outside institutions, she still felt helplessly lost if she took a wrong turn at the end of a block.

Now she tried not to think too much about Sassy's navigating the Boston streets with one hand on the steering wheel and the other on the phone.

"Hi, Mr. Misra—"

Sassy winced, no doubt getting an earful from Erin's father. She couldn't make out the words, but she could pick up some of the tone.

A minute later, Sassy managed to say, "Yes, sir," before Erin's father went off again. Thirty or so seconds more passed before Sassy said sharply, "I can't drive her home if I don't know where your house is, so please, spare me the lecture until we're there. Or we can keep chatting while I hop on the highway at seventy miles an hour." Frowning, he listened a minute more. "Yeah, I'll be taking I-90. Uh-huh. Okay . . . run that street name by me again? Okay, that's easy enough. We should be there in half an hour."

He flipped the phone closed and handed it over without looking away from the road.

"I think your dad is cross with me."

"Uh-*huh*." Awkwardly, Erin added, "So. You had stuff to say."

"Yeah . . . ," he said, his voice barely audible.

Could *Sassy* really be at a loss for words? Unnerved, Erin prodded. "Well? Spill. We aren't getting any farther from home."

"Mhmm." They merged onto the highway, and at last, Sassy started to talk. "Remember you asked me, why the lies?"

"Yes?"

"You're not going to believe me," he said. "Not right away. But I told you I'd tell you."

"So go ahead," Erin said impatiently.

"Fine. Here goes."

Erin waited with unveiled skepticism as he once more drummed out a prologue on the steering wheel.

"I was twelve when things started to go weird for me. I was at summer camp in Maine, in the woods. There came this beautiful night, with a full moon. We were making s'mores, but I was . . . insanely restless. I managed to wander away from the others. I needed to stretch my legs. I found myself pretty deep in the woods, and that's when it happened for the first time."

"When *what* happened?"

"I changed."

"Changed . . . how?"

"Changed my body. Changed into an animal." Erin started to protest, but he rushed on. "After that, sometimes I could do it, and sometimes I couldn't. I needed to at least be able to see the moon to—"

"Sassy," Erin sighed. How could he possibly think that all

this would help convince her of whatever strange truth he meant to impart?

It occurred to her that maybe Sassy wasn't capable of telling her the truth. Maybe whatever had happened—perhaps even when he was twelve and at summer camp—was so horrible that his mind had made up this lie. She had heard that kind of theory a lot, as doctors tried to get her to confess some horrible secret in her own background to explain her otherwise inexplicable condition.

"Tell me, Erin," Sassy asked, "how does a diagnosed compulsive liar convince *anyone* of *anything*?"

"Damned if I know," she grumbled. "Tell me more, then."

"You don't believe me."

"Of course I don't believe you. You said I wouldn't. Maybe you should tell me the part you think relates to *me* before we get home."

He tapped his hand anxiously on the steering wheel. "How do I reason with someone who doesn't trust her own mind? Or show the truth to someone who doesn't trust her own *senses*?"

She wasn't sure whether she wanted to encourage him to try, just to see what he would say. They drove in silence for a while as she tried to decide. Erin rubbed her temples, still feeling hazy from the drugs—but not so hazy that she failed to notice when they pulled into a familiar parking lot.

"This is the school. Sassy, you jerk, *why* are we at the school?"

He came to a stop a bit too abruptly for comfort and snapped the car into park.

"I'm pretty well established as unreliable when it comes to the truth," Sassy said as Erin shoved open the door, planning to put a little distance between them and then call her father.

Sassy got out but didn't come after her.

Was that . . . Oh, thank *god*. Erin didn't know why Marissa was at school hours before it opened for the day, but she had rarely been more grateful to see anyone in her life.

Chapter 13

SHEVAUN PACED AROUND THE ROOM, leaving dents in the wall when she tapped a hand against it at each turn.

"You're telling me I can't go near the girl," she said flatly. "Even though she has the ability to *possess* me, even though on occasion she opens her eyes with *my* memories behind them, even though she could have who knows what information, I still need to ask someone's permission to go near her?"

Adjila winced—with good reason—as Shevaun's voice rose. She had taken down empires in this kind of mood, slaughtered whole lineages, and wrought bloody havoc across continents.

"I'm saying," he replied carefully, "that someone has a claim on her. The drugs in her blood have muddled the power signature too much for me to clearly read it, but if I had to make a guess, I would say someone tried to train her as a Triste."

"Your kind doesn't give up its students to madhouses and drugs," Shevaun argued. "*Your* teacher nearly killed me the first time I dared talk to you. This Erin doesn't even seem to know we exist, and she has no one openly protecting her."

"Sometimes the training goes bad, especially with certain teachers." He spoke the words neutrally, but this time it was Shevaun's turn to wince at how dense she had been.

Tristes varied in how they went about training their chosen. Some spent years with a student. There was even one, named Tatiana, who worked across generations, gradually building the tolerance and magic in a family until a child who suited her came along. But Adjila's teacher, Pandora, believed in the swiftest, harshest teaching methods, those which created the strongest witches . . . but had the highest fatality rate.

Shevaun had met perhaps twoscore of Pandora's students over the half millennium she had traveled with Adjila. Of all those, she knew of only two survivors.

Most died abruptly, as blood vessels burst in their brains or hearts. Some died slowly, as other organs collapsed and their bodies stopped functioning. One went blind and then deaf, and then he simply stopped responding to anything at all until Pandora broke his neck to keep him from starving.

"So you think the girl might have been abandoned after the training went awry," Shevaun said. Adjila had withdrawn to the window; another woman might have reached for him, but Shevaun knew better.

"It's possible," he replied. "It might have happened when she was a child, someone working on a variation of Tatiana's techniques, in which case Erin's whole story about being institutionalized since she was young might be correct. Or it might have happened more recently, and the teacher in question manipulated some human man's memories so he would accept her as his daughter. Either way, Erin's own memories of the training could easily have been . . . removed."

The removal of memories seemed a curious coincidence in this case. "Might those memories have been replaced by other ones?" she asked. Shevaun had never studied witch magics, but she had spent centuries with Adjila. She knew that sometimes meddling with the mind had unforeseen consequences. "Especially if her teacher were someone close to you, could that have acted as . . ." She fumbled for the right words to describe such an effect.

"It's possible I acted as a bridge to you, if someone close to me is responsible. Maybe they meant to form the connection between me and the girl but it slipped to you because your mind is more susceptible to Triste magic. It might even have been entirely accidental; stranger things have happened when my kind has 'experimented.' " He frowned. "Or it could have been intentional, in which case it was done by someone more powerful than I, and the girl is bait. We don't lack for enemies."

"Mmm." The thought of someone more powerful than Adjila, and thus more powerful than Shevaun, wasn't fun. She knew such people *existed,* but as a rule she didn't care to think about them.

"You have absolutely no memory of ever waking up as this girl?" Adjila asked. "And nothing strange happened to you earlier, when she switched over?"

"I think I would recall waking up as a human," Shevaun replied. "I was hunting when you went to play. Nothing unusual happened. What does that mean?"

"I don't know yet," Adjila said. "One way or another, I think it would be a bad idea to get too close until we know whose power she's marked with, how and why the connection between you was made, and what the consequences of harming her might be. If she has been abandoned, we should be able to identify her teacher and get permission to help clean up this little mess, but it's rude to intrude until then."

"How is it *rude?*" Shevaun protested. "They walked off without her, and now she's giving us trouble."

"Even *if* she was abandoned, she was still once a student. Pandora routinely kills her own students, but you may have noticed that she doesn't fancy having other people interfere with them. Among my kind, you simply . . . don't."

Adjila usually ignored the social norms of his own kind. He had refused to let them get in his way when he had fallen for Shevaun, so it frustrated her that he felt the need to indulge them now.

"It would be trouble. If it's a mistake, we'll clean it up, and if it's not a mistake, we don't want to charge in until we know who we're dealing with."

Shevaun nodded, though not without a certain resentment. "So you'll speak to the other Tristes."

"I'll speak to Pandora when I go back to meet with her. If something is going on among our kind, she usually knows about it."

"And if no one admits to it?"

"Then we clear the drugs out of her system so I can read the power on her, and decide how to go from there."

Shevaun growled. "And in the *meantime?*"

"In the meantime, it's after sunrise," Adjila said. "Can we get some sleep?"

Instead, Shevaun returned to pacing. "I don't want to sleep."

She couldn't kill the girl, which was what she *really* wanted to do. At least Adjila had had a chance to play with her a bit before he had noticed the power on her and backed off. Shevaun had only gone so far as to see a photo album, and that alone . . .

She wrapped her arms across her chest.

Adjila put a hand on her shoulder. "You're exhausted, Shevaun. You still aren't fully recovered from your injuries—"

"I won't *be* fully recovered until we get rid of this *pest.*"

"You're afraid to sleep."

She pulled away. "I'm going to hunt."

"You need to sleep sometime," he said in his damnably calm voice.

"*You* try sleeping!" she shouted. "You try closing your eyes, knowing someone else might take you over. . . ." She snarled. "I'm going to hunt again. Then maybe I'll sleep. Or maybe I'll kill the girl and get it over with."

· He grabbed her arm. "Don't do anything rash. You kill her and it might kill *you*," he reminded her. "Or whoever she belongs to might come after all of us—not just you and me, but Brittany and Iana, too."

That made Shevaun hesitate, for the moment. She leaned back against the wall.

"I feel *wrong*," she pronounced. "Ever since I looked at those pictures, I've felt . . ." She struggled for words. "Like something is scratching at my brain. I tried to hunt, and I tried to paint, and I tried to explore the city, but nothing felt like me."

She never would have admitted that to anyone else. She didn't even like saying it around Adjila, but she needed him to understand why she couldn't rest without having done anything to make this *right*.

"Okay," Adjila said. "We'll go looking for Pandora now, then. Maybe she'll have some answers for us."

Shevaun shook her head. "Not at this hour. You know as well as I do that she won't even let us in the door this early in the day."

"If things are this bad, then I'll convince her. I've faced her wrath before."

* * *

Half an hour later, they stood on the doorstep of Pandora's main estate in New Hampshire, and Shevaun remembered why she usually avoided going there.

First there was the fact that Pandora shielded her territory from everyone but her students, the very few people she liked, and the even fewer people capable of overpowering her. Shevaun was not on any of those lists, so visiting Pandora meant letting Adjila drive.

Second, though they had been together for half a thousand years, Pandora still disapproved of her favorite student's relationship with a vampire. Because of this, Shevaun tended to regard Pandora as a particularly dangerous mother-in-law. That only added to Pandora's ire, since Pandora had been Adjila's *first* lover and did not like being treated like an old hag.

On the other hand, Shevaun knew that Pandora's powers of politics and networking were profound. Shevaun had never had the patience to keep up with the world, whereas Pandora not only kept a finger in every worthwhile pie, she was apt to be baking the most important ones. In that way, she had much in common with the vampire who had changed Shevaun. Theron claimed to have been actively involved in the rise and fall of every major empire since the founding of Tenochtitlán and the Aztec Triple Alliance.

Adjila had not even raised his hand to knock when the

front door was opened from within by another witch who had been initiated a couple of centuries after Adjila.

This day keeps getting better and better! Shevaun thought. She and this whelp, Alexander, had had a bit of a run-in a while back—something about her renouncing the Devil. It had been the last religious argument she had had the poor sense to get into.

"Is Pandora up?" Adjila asked.

Alexander shook his head. "Not at this hour."

Adjila frowned at his little-brother-by-magic. Slender, with golden eyes and hair, Alexander usually had a complexion that was fair but not pale. That day, though, he looked haggard, his skin a shade too gray to be healthy and his cheeks hollow.

"If she wakes and finds you in this condition—"

Alexander stepped back, interrupting Adjila by saying, "You might as well wait in the library. She has a noon meeting, so she should be up early."

"We'll wait," Adjila agreed, still watching Alexander closely. "You should feed."

"I will," he replied, glancing hungrily at Shevaun.

"Don't look at *me* like that," Shevaun snapped.

Alexander sighed. "Did she have to come?"

"Yes," Adjila replied bluntly, no longer solicitous. He wrapped an arm around Shevaun's waist and led the way toward the library.

"What is he doing here?" Shevaun grumbled. "The boy is three hundred years old. Didn't he move out of Mommy's house a long time ago?"

"Sometimes the birds come back to the nest awhile," Adjila replied vaguely.

"*You* never did."

"That's because I had the sense to realize that Pandora is a sadist and a sociopath." The sound of a woman clearing her throat made Shevaun tense, but Adjila simply turned to greet his maker. "Pandora, you're up early."

"I was worried Alexander might eat your hussy," Pandora replied. "What brings you two to my parlor at this time of day? I had thought France would amuse you at least a while more. Surely those hunters didn't scare you off?"

Barely over the threshold and Shevaun already felt on the defensive. Pandora always knew too much. She gritted her teeth and looked toward the many leather-bound volumes Pandora kept in her library, using them as an excuse not to speak. Adjila could handle the conversation.

"We've stumbled across a girl who, the best I can tell, has been partially trained as one of us. I'm trying to figure out who might have a claim on her," he said.

"The best you can tell?" Pandora repeated. "What's the problem?"

"She has been so heavily medicated it is nearly impossible to read her," he explained. "She and her human father seem to think she is mad. She goes by the name Erin Misrahe, and lives in Massachusetts."

"Erin . . ." Pandora paused to think, then shook her head. "No one in our line has been dealing with anyone like that recently. I suppose I could inquire with some of the other lines. Any particular reason?"

"We've run into her a couple of times. I wanted to make sure we weren't stepping on any toes," Adjila replied. "Though as long as I'm here, I will admit I'm curious as to what brings Alexander home."

Shevaun knew he brought this up to keep Pandora from becoming too curious about recent events with Erin.

Pandora tossed her head. "Family troubles. You know that boy. It's a miracle if he can decide what he wants for *dinner,* much less out of his life."

"He's powerful, but he's soft," Adjila said. "And he looks like he hasn't fed in days."

"I'm aware," Pandora said, voice low. "He and I disagreed on a recent project of mine. Apparently the outcome upset him."

Shevaun idled while Adjila made polite conversation for a few minutes more and then gratefully allowed Pandora to escort them to the front door.

"Well," Adjila said once they were outside again, "either she doesn't know a thing, or she's responsible."

"I'll bet you a puppy it's the second choice," Shevaun grumbled. "It wouldn't be the first time she's tried to kill me."

"Erin is more of an overt danger to me than to you," Adjila said. "As long as you don't attempt to injure her just yet, at least. And since when have you wanted a puppy?"

Shevaun shrugged. "Alexander always reminds me of some kind of abused golden retriever. It makes me want a dog."

"Let's wait to try to housebreak an animal until after we deal with Erin, shall we?"

"Never mind the dog." She flicked a ladybug off her shoulder. Why did Pandora have to have so many *plants* around her front walk? "I still think Pandora did this. It resembles one of her experiments, and she doesn't hesitate to put her students in danger."

"Normally, I would agree," Adjila said, "but Pandora's experiments are usually more controlled than this. There are enough people surrounding Erin, including her shapeshifter friend, that I think Pandora would find it . . . messy."

"Hmm." Shevaun wasn't the type to prefer logic to an easy grudge, but sadly, she wasn't completely blind to reason, either.

However, even if she could not interfere with Erin quite yet, there was nothing keeping her from Erin's little friend Sassy, with his bad pickup lines. Or had he actually recognized her, from his relationship with Erin? For that matter, had she recognized *him*? She recalled the strange compulsion that had sent her into that particular café, after she had passed a dozen others in her walk.

She shook the thoughts away before she became too paranoid. For now she had to believe she was making choices of her own free will. Otherwise the human girl wouldn't be the only one who would be mad.

"I've decided I want a puppy now after all," Shevaun announced. Even if she couldn't fix all her problems, at least she could make dinner plans.

Chapter 14

"I AM SO GLAD to see you," Erin said as she approached Marissa. It was only six in the morning, an hour and a half before the public school day began, but maybe Marissa was always this early. "I know this is random, but do you think you could give me a ride home?"

Marissa glanced at Sassy, who was still standing by his car. "Be glad *after* I talk to you," Marissa said softly.

"If this is related to whatever issue you and Sassy have going on, can it wait until I get home?" Erin pleaded.

"I'm here because Sassy called me when you were sleeping," Marissa said. "You had my number in your phone. This whole thing is my fault. I should have explained, not just—"

"For the record, I agree it's *your* fault," Sassy said in an ice-cold voice. Erin jumped, not having realized that he had come up behind her. "But that's hardly the important part."

"To hell with this," Erin said, and pulled her phone out of her pocket.

"Erin, wait," Marissa called.

"Hi, Dad. It's Erin. I'm going to need a ride from the public school."

"The *school*?"

"Yeah. Can you pick me up?"

"I'll be there right away. Are you safe for the moment?"

Erin glanced at the others. "I think so," she answered. "Just . . . come soon. Love you, Dad."

"Sassy, what did you *tell* her?" Marissa was demanding.

"What you *didn't*!" Sassy shouted. "You let Erin *see* you, and you just went right on letting her think she was crazy."

"Oh, and you told her years ago, did you?"

"I didn't know what I was when I first met her!" he spat back. "I would still be in that hospital, thinking I was crazy, if not for her."

"Stop it!" Erin shouted. "I don't know whose idea this little joke was, but it isn't *funny*!"

"No, it isn't," Marissa said. "Erin, I know what you're going through. This has been handled really badly, but please, sit down a second and let me talk, okay?"

"I don't want to talk," Erin said. "I want to go home, and I want to go to sleep. And I want to wake up and . . ." *Have all this be a dream.* But did she really?

She had had an episode after dinner with Sassy. Now, the next morning, here were her friends, acting completely crazy. Or was it her? Marissa didn't seem the type for practical jokes, especially ones this cruel, and Sassy had never taken his issues out on her. Was it possible that Erin wasn't even hearing what they were actually saying?

Possible. Very, very bad, and absolutely possible.

With trembling hands, Erin dialed her doctor's pager and left her number. Then she crumpled to the ground, pulling her knees to her chest and resting her forehead on them. She would just stay *right here* until her father arrived.

Marissa sat beside her and started talking in the tone one would use to coax a skittish cat out from under a couch. Erin tried not to listen.

"There are a lot of things that exist in this world that most people don't know about," Marissa said. "Most people don't *want* to know about them. I should have told you the truth about me after you saw me change, but I thought maybe you would be better off not knowing. Given how hard you said change was for you, I thought it would be easier for you to just go on being innocent."

Marissa waited a moment for Erin to speak, but when Erin kept her head down, she continued anyway.

"You told me your medications have been stable for a while now. So I hope maybe you'll trust yourself, at least a little. And that you'll trust *me,* a whole lot. Because I . . . well, I'm a shapeshifter. Most of the time I look human. Sometimes I look like a tiger. But I'm still me, either way." She paused. "Sassy is some kind of shapeshifter, too. We can usually sense the power on each other, though it's hard to tell breed. . . ." She sighed. "Erin, would you *look* at me, please?"

Erin focused instead on taking deep breaths. Her father would be there soon.

"The point is, there are a lot of people, probably plenty you've met, who aren't completely human. Most of them act just like anyone else. They go to school. They pay taxes. All that stuff."

This was ridiculous. "Marissa," Erin said, gritting her teeth, "I know you're trying . . ." What did she know? Never mind that. "Just leave me alone."

"You don't have to believe me now," Marissa replied. "I just want you to have some information that you can think over if—"

"Marissa. *Please.* You don't know—"

"*I* know," Sassy said, sitting beside her. "I know you're scared of losing yourself. I know you're scared of not knowing what's real and what's not. And I know that right now you're scared you're having an attack and might hurt someone. But you're not. Because you're strong."

He put a hand on her arm, and Erin didn't have the energy to push him away.

"I'm sorry I scared you," he whispered. "But I wanted to . . . Erin, you probably saved my life, back when we were in the ward together. I would never hurt you."

"Then why are you saying these things to me?" she whispered.

"Because you were the first person who didn't call me a

liar," he said. "You thought you were just hallucinating, but you saw me for what I was. Just the fact that *someone* had—" He ran a hand through his hair, mussing it. "Well, I had to talk to you. And you said something then that I'll never forget: you said that you didn't care if everyone out there thought you were wrong, as long as you were *sure* about what you believed to be true. It's what got me through, and made me realize that I didn't need to convince other people that I was right and they were wrong. I just needed to convince myself. You did that for me. I just . . ." He squeezed her hand. "You'll be okay, Erin. Please, just trust me."

Chapter 15

SHEVAUN HAD NO INTENTION of *harming* anyone, but when she discovered Erin out and about after she parted ways with Adjila, Shevaun couldn't resist perching on the roof of the schoolhouse to observe her.

For an innocent, ignorant little girl, Erin certainly kept interesting company. She was currently sitting on the asphalt, leaning against the tasty hyena shapeshifter while another shapeshifter they called Marissa talked to her.

"What will you do now?" Marissa asked.

Erin took a deep breath and said, "Hospital."

"You don't *need* a hospital," the puppy said. "Erin, please, you have to—"

"I'm not *safe* here," Erin snapped. "I'm not, and other people aren't. You know that, Sassy."

While Erin and Sassy had cuddled, Marissa had pulled out a cell phone, and she now hit a single number.

"SingleEarth Haven number four," a voice on the other end of the line answered.

Shevaun shook her head with disdain. SingleEarth had been established to create a peaceful place where humans, vampires, shapeshifters, and witches of all kinds could co-exist. Its mission of peace was supported by a global coalition of doctors, scientists, teachers, safe houses, libraries, laboratories, and hospitals. Despite its cheerful goals, the group had dangerous enemies, so it was protected by a small army of vampire hunters and a handful of powerful independent mercenaries—including, unfortunately, people like Pandora.

"This is Marissa kuloka Mari," the shapeshifter said. The form of name indicated that she was Mistari—a tiger shapeshifter—but the surname was used only by those who did not claim affiliation with any specific tribe. Shevaun wasn't surprised, since Mistari law forbade children to leave their homeland or associate with humans. Marissa had probably been taken in by SingleEarth after her own people disowned her.

"I'm currently at the Nefershen High School. I need you to pull psychiatric and medical records for Erin Misrahe."

Erin's father arrived while Marissa was still on the phone; he barely put his car into park before hurrying to Erin's side. Sassy backed off when the older man glared at him, but father and daughter exchanged only a few words.

"Are you okay?"

She shook her head.

"Do we need to go to the hospital?"

A pause, ever so brief, and then Erin nodded. She trembled a little as she walked toward the car without looking back at her friends.

"Don't worry," Marissa said to Sassy as she closed her phone. "I called the local SingleEarth chapter. They'll—"

Shevaun had lost interest and was about to leave when the hyena puppy suddenly turned about, fire in his eyes, and growled, "You *what?*"

Marissa took a nervous step back but sounded more confused than defensive when she answered, "I called SingleEarth. They can look through Erin's psychiatric records, and if there's a magical issue in addition to a human one, they'll be able to help her. They'll also explain about us, and help her accept that—"

"You smug, self-righteous, paternalistic *cat.*"

Shevaun, perched on the school rooftop, smiled at the particular string of invectives. Darling Sassy apparently wasn't fond of coloring inside the lines.

"What is your *problem?*" Marissa snapped in response. "Human doctors won't be able to—"

"SingleEarth." He spat the name like a bad word. "Any help SingleEarth will give her will practically be an afterthought. They don't understand what's going on any better than human doctors do; they just have more options to choose from."

"Which means they are better equipped to find out what's really the problem," Marissa argued.

"More than anything in the world, Erin wants to be normal. She wants to be safe," Sassy said. "If SingleEarth finds out that she has witch DNA, or shapeshifter, or something else odd, they won't let her be those things. They'll want to involve her in all their causes and they'll strong-arm her into learning to use whatever abilities she is supposed to have, without any respect for her desire to just be *human*."

"If she has power—"

"The only power she wants," Sassy insisted, "is the power to control her own mind. SingleEarth will dump information on her and talk about the power she could have, and the abilities she might have, and the *choices she has to make,* and they won't understand that she is still afraid to go to sleep because she might wake up somewhere else. They will keep her from talking to any of the therapists she knows and trusts because they don't know the 'truth.' They'll even discourage her from talking to her father. They will rip away every safety net she has and then say, 'You're free now. You're cured.' "

"They'll stay with her until she *is* cured, of whatever needs curing," Marissa said, sounding impatient. "They'll make sure she's safe before releasing her, just like any hospital would."

"Safe by their definition."

He started to turn away, but Marissa grabbed his arm.

"Sassy, what *happened* to you?" she asked. "I work with

SingleEarth because I agree with their views on compassion and acceptance, *and* their methods of education. If someone there hurt you, then that should be reported. If there's something wrong with the system—"

He shook his head and pulled out of her grip. "None of your business."

"I assume your parents were human?" Marissa called after him, obviously trying to divine his history.

Shevaun's only real issue with SingleEarth was that it was an organization, with its own political system, and Shevaun had never been much of a team player. She was curious about how it had wronged this boy.

"Erin said she saw you turn into a tiger," Sassy said, pausing before he got to his car. "You're Mistari, right?"

Marissa nodded.

"They're pretty isolationist. I imagine you were born to two Mistari parents, raised by your own kind?"

"My tribe is in exile," she answered, "but yes, I was raised knowing what I was. I know how hard it can be to learn later in life, though. I've met a lot of people through the haven whose parents carried a shapeshifter gene without knowing it. It's common in—"

"Common in the American population. I know," he interrupted. "That's what SingleEarth said, when I asked them why my parents didn't warn me. My breed is apparently among the most common to be carried recessively by otherwise human parents. Or so they told me."

"You're Pakana?" Marissa asked sympathetically. "I'm sorry. I know—"

"You do not *know*!" Sassy glared at her. "SingleEarth had my file from the time I was fifteen. Shortly after I checked into the ward where I met Erin, a doctor there reported my case to them. I didn't know that at the time, of course. In fact, I didn't learn it until later, when someone finally found the buried report with a note on it saying 'No counselors available at this time. Subject safe enough in current location.' "

" 'Safe enough'?" Marissa repeated incredulously. "I've seen the kind of self-inflicted wounds that human-raised Pakana come in with. No one at SingleEarth would have left—"

"Two years," Sassy said flatly. "I spent months in the ward before I managed to deceive the doctors well enough for them to proclaim me safe, and then it was two years more before SingleEarth remembered me. They apologized for taking so long. Called it a misfile."

"Oh, my god," the tiger whispered.

Shevaun understood Marissa's horror. Only a few breeds of shapeshifters—the hyenas, the wolves, and the cougars—were affected by the full moon. Of those three, Pakana were the most compelled to change; if they couldn't, either because they didn't know how or because they were not in a safe location, they tended to dig into their own skins, cutting themselves to somehow relieve the pressure. Without the assistance of other Pakana, hyenas often never learned to shapeshift. Come adolescence, the moon brought about the need to change, but not the ability.

Many human-raised Pakana killed themselves, or others, before they could ever learn control.

Shevaun scowled, standing and stretching, as she realized she was dangerously close to pitying the boy. He was in love with Erin; that much was obvious. But Shevaun might need to destroy Erin, which meant that caring for Sassy was useless, and even dangerous.

So, his history had been rough. There was no use feeling sorry about that when she might have to make his present or his future a whole lot worse.

Chapter 16

ERIN HATED HOSPITAL WAITING ROOMS. Fortunately, she tended not to linger in them too long.

"Are you thinking of harming yourself or others?" the emergency room nurse asked without glancing up from the routine psych form.

"Not *yet*," Erin replied, which made the nurse's eyes widen. "But since 'history of violent behavior' is written about five hundred times in my record, it shouldn't surprise you when it happens."

That was one way to get quick treatment. It wasn't long before she got her very own bed in a section of the hospital that only opened with a special key and pass. Her father made sure she was settled, and then left to pack her clothes and other necessary belongings from home while she spoke to the doctors. He'd offered to stay, but Erin had been through this process too many times before to need his help.

The first doctor she got to see said the same thing countless others had said before him: "Someone your size and age doesn't need such high dosages of any of these medications." He made the pronouncement as he looked through the sack of prescription bottles she had checked in with.

"Last time they dropped my medications, I stuck a pencil through a nurse's hand. Really want to try it?" Her mood was not improved by the fact that she was seeing hazy colors all around her again. Her father had given her that morning's medication in the car, but the missed dose of the night before, along with the stress, was taking its toll. "Look, talk to my other doctors. They can give you my whole history, if you don't believe my file."

A knock on the door made the doctor frown. "Yes?"

Two more men walked in. One was older and wearing a name tag that indicated he was a supervisor. The second man looked like he was in his late thirties, and he didn't have a name tag. He was dressed in a suit instead of scrubs, but he carried the obligatory clipboard under his arm.

The haze around him was mellow blue-green, which at least was nicer than the other colors in the room. Erin blinked, trying to clear the miasma of hallucination from the figure, without success.

"Frank, this is Isaac Francisco," the supervisor said to Erin's doctor. "He's a specialist from Chivalry Psychiatric. Erin, Dr. Francisco would like a few minutes of your time."

Erin's doctor seemed surprised, but he shook hands with the new doctor as Erin watched in confusion.

"What's going on?" she asked.

"Good morning, Erin," Dr. Francisco said as the others left. He sat down in a chair by her bedside. "How are you doing?"

"Crazy, apparently," she replied sharply. "My regular psychologist is already on her way. Why are you here?" She had never even heard of Chivalry Psychiatric, and she was familiar with most of the psych resources in the area.

He cleared his throat. "I should introduce myself more fully. I specialize in a condition called acute psychorizia, which is a rare ailment that is often misdiagnosed due to lack of awareness in the general medical community."

"Someone thinks I might have been misdiagnosed? For eight years?" Erin asked, incredulous. "I find that hard to believe."

"Your first psychiatrist reluctantly diagnosed you with schizophrenia after learning you had suffered perinatal hypoxia, which is correlated with schizophrenia. Do you know what that means?"

Erin blinked. "Hypoxia is oxygen deprivation. Perinatal would mean around the time of birth. I read a lot of psychology books. What happened?"

"I do not know how much your father may have told you, but there were complications during your birth," the doctor replied. "Your mother was in an accident, and you were delivered in an emergency cesarean section, seven weeks early. You stopped breathing several times."

"I knew my mother died during childbirth," Erin said softly. Her father had told her when she was old enough to ask and understand the answer, but he had never mentioned Erin had come to losing her own life. "That kind of complication makes sense with my diagnosis, doesn't it?"

"It would," he replied, "and previous doctors have certainly believed it *does.* But while it might be a convenient diagnosis, your MRI and PET scans don't support it. Neither does your ability to pick up languages; *j'ai appris que vous parlez français et latin?*"

I understand that you speak French and Latin? "Yes, I—hey!" She had understood the French as easily as she did English.

"There was no damage to your brain, or your intelligence, as far as we can tell. You suffer none of the language disabilities common in children with schizophrenia, and you report no sense of alienation or isolation beyond what is perfectly reasonable for someone raised in the conditions you have been."

"I've had a lot of doctors tell me it's not a classic case, which is why it's so hard to figure out how to treat it," Erin said, "but once they ruled out things like drugs and brain cancer, it was all that was left."

He shook his head. "With your father's and your permission, I would like to have you transferred to a specialized facility, where we can run the necessary tests to hopefully get you a *correct* diagnosis, and with it an appropriate treatment plan."

She frowned and said honestly, "I've never heard of Chivalry Psychiatric, or . . . acute psychorizia. How did my case come to your attention?" She had been in and out of hospitals for too long to be optimistic about any miracle cure.

"Chivalry is one branch of an organization known as SingleEarth. One of your friends works for . . . You're frowning."

She *was* frowning. It seemed strange that she had never heard of SingleEarth during her eight years of symptoms, and had now heard of it twice in twenty-four hours. She remembered how tense Sassy had been about it; how he had described SingleEarth as a kind of "new age" hospital. Maybe she was a cynic, but she preferred the old-fashioned, biomedical approach to chanting and crystals.

"Do you have some information my father and I could look at, on both the condition you're talking about and the hospital?" Erin asked. If it was a private, alternative facility, they would have some kind of advertising brochure, which would help her figure out how legitimate they were. Obviously they were respected within the medical community, or the hospital wouldn't have let Dr. Francisco in to see her. And yet Sassy's take on it still made her skeptical.

She fully recognized the irony in how much she trusted a self-admitted compulsive liar who hated doctors and all other authority figures.

Dr. Francisco nodded and obligingly produced a stapled, folded sheaf of papers. "Some basic information on

SingleEarth, and psychorizia." He glanced over his shoulder, at the hallway. "I'll give you some time to read that, and be back tomorrow. In the meantime, it looks like your friend Marissa is here, if you're up for visitors. She's the one who recognized your condition and called us."

Erin started to shake her head but then changed her mind. How had Marissa, of all people—the only friend Erin hadn't met in a hospital—come to know about this strange, ultrarare illness that Erin had never heard of? "I'll see her."

Dr. Francisco said his polite goodbyes and nodded for Marissa to come in as he left.

"I'm so sorry, Erin," Marissa said as she sank into the chair. "I just want to say that. I'm sorry."

"Nothing for you to be sorry for," Erin said awkwardly. She knew that seeing an illness in action made it more real, and more devastating, but she didn't have much energy to spare to comfort anyone else at the moment.

"Dr. Francisco can help you. Really. I should have called him weeks ago." Marissa bit her lip.

"He left me some information to read," Erin said, hoisting the papers. Regardless of whether Erin chose to go with SingleEarth, she hoped they were helping Marissa.

She was grateful when she saw Tina in the hall. Erin lifted a hand and waved. "My doctor's here," she said.

"Oh!" Marissa stood up, her arms across her chest. "Well, you have my number. Call me to let me know how you're doing."

Erin nodded. "I will."

"Sassy should be here a little later," Marissa said. "He and I had a bit of an . . . argument . . . but he's serious about wanting to take care of you. Apparently he stayed awake all last night while you were asleep, to make sure you didn't run off. I made him promise to get a couple hours' rest before he took his car back on the highway . . . though I think he only agreed because he knew you wouldn't have much time to see him yet."

"Thanks." Erin smiled a little, imagining what it would take for Sassy to accept advice from anyone.

Marissa nearly bumped into Tina on her way out. Erin shook her head, but her concern about Marissa faded when she saw Tina's calm but serious expression. She could worry all she liked about other people, but eventually she had to face the fact that she was the one in the biggest trouble.

Chapter 17

Adjila woke with a start as Shevaun dropped with a bounce onto the edge of the bed where he'd been sleeping.

"Your girl," Shevaun announced, "not only spends time with some unusual friends, she has now checked herself into a hospital."

"*My* girl, is she now?" Adjila replied with a yawn and a glance out the window. "You said you were going to pick up the puppy—and that you were going to leave Erin alone."

"I said I wouldn't kill her or hurt her," Shevaun said, correcting him. "I didn't."

Adjila ran his hands along his hair as he sat up. He had just barely fallen asleep. He had hoped Shevaun would join him and finally get some *rest* instead of dragging him out of bed again at barely an hour past sunset.

"So. She's in a hospital," he said, still groggy. "Which one?"

"For the moment, a human one," Shevaun answered,

"but she has a little friend, a tiger associated with SingleEarth, who—"

"A tiger?" Adjila asked, now wide awake.

Shevaun nodded sharply, obviously not interested in the particulars.

"A tiger, yes, who called SingleEarth. They'll take one look at her file and see my name, and I don't want anyone experimenting on her after that."

Adjila shook his head; the SingleEarth issue was not his main concern. "Do you know what tribe the tiger is from?" he asked. Shevaun shot him an annoyed look. He clarified. "The shapeshifters in the hunters' group in Sète were tigers."

Her eyes widened, and she smiled a little. "*Really?* Now, that is a fascinating coincidence."

After five hundred years, Shevaun believed in chaos and the occasional cruelty of fate, but Adjila knew that the artist in her tended to see form and pattern amid all that bedlam. She did not believe in coincidence.

"Let's pick up Erin first," Adjila said, planning as he spoke. "We want to get to her before she is in SingleEarth's custody."

He had hoped to figure out who Erin was *before* he risked offending her possible protectors, but that wasn't an option anymore. SingleEarth was dedicated to peace, but they defended themselves strongly, and they disliked Shevaun and Adjila. They might see the girl as more than a human to save; she could be a weapon.

"We should talk to the tiger, too. Marissa," Shevaun said,

with a strange, distracted expression. "I wonder how she's related to the tigers we killed."

"The tigers who tried to kill *you*, you mean?" Adjila said.

Shevaun nodded and then frowned. "Of course. I'm just tired. You know how that makes me . . . sentimental."

Adjila frowned. Normally when Shevaun was tired, she was exactly the opposite, in fact—cranky, violent, and prone to psychopathic, destructive rages. He didn't mention it, though.

"Maybe you should stay here and rest while I go get Erin," he suggested. If Marissa was a hunter, he didn't want Shevaun near her until she was stronger and less emotional.

Shevaun reinforced Adjila's concerns when she added, "If you see the puppy, bring him, too. He's fun."

"Sure," Adjila said. "You lie down."

She shrugged. "Maybe when you get back. I'll let the girls know what's going on, and then I think I have an idea for a painting."

Thank god. When Shevaun had oils in front of her, she could be distracted for days or weeks, long enough for him to try to sort out what was causing her strange behavior.

Adjila found his way to Erin's local hospital, then slipped easily past security and through the locked corridors.

Amusingly, he almost ran right into one of SingleEarth's foremost doctors in the hallway outside the psychiatric wing. "Doctor" Isaac Francisco's medical license was as false as the birth certificates and social security numbers SingleEarth often provided for individuals whose inability to age made it difficult for them to function in the modern world. He paled upon seeing Adjila.

"I see my reputation proceeds me," Adjila said as the supposed doctor stopped short.

"Are you the one who has been giving me trouble?" Isaac asked.

A curious question. "I do not believe I have given you any trouble *yet*," Adjila answered. Noticing the file under the man's arm, he asked, "Is that Erin's?"

He held out a hand for it.

Isaac hesitated, apparently trying to take the moral high ground, but then his sense of self-preservation seemed to kick in and prompted him to turn it over.

"She was first reported to SingleEarth eight years ago," Isaac said, "but someone put a mark on her file saying it wasn't relevant to us. She was reported again three years ago, but somehow she 'mysteriously' fell through the cracks again then, too, along with the young man mentioned in the same report. If that was your doing—"

"Not mine," Adjila admitted. "If you can track down who it was, though, that would be useful."

The list of people capable of manipulating SingleEarth was short, but it included both Shevaun's sire, Theron, and Adjila's teacher, Pandora. Adjila could picture either of them making an effort to keep a girl with such a strange connection to Shevaun out of SingleEarth's hands.

Adjila planned to speak to both of them.

"You do not have the medical or psychiatric background necessary to help this girl," Isaac said, growing a spine at last. "Please, let SingleEarth address her case."

In response, Adjila put a hand on the door to the psychiatric ward.

"You need a nurse inside to open—"

Isaac stopped talking when Adjila sent a bolt of power into the door, shorting out the electric circuits that controlled the lock.

"Thanks for the information," Adjila said. Then he paused and asked, "What can you tell me about the tiger Marissa?"

"I don't see why that's any of your business," Isaac replied.

"And I don't see why anyone at SingleEarth would blame you for answering my questions, when they surely have a lengthy file on me detailing the kinds of things I'm capable of doing to people who annoy me."

He spoke calmly. Shevaun's fiery rage was beautiful, but Adjila's quiet control could be just as effective, painful, or deadly, as he chose.

Isaac swallowed tightly. "Her tribe was exiled from the homeland when she was a young child," he said, "but they mostly maintained Mistari culture. She chose to accept SingleEarth's offer of shelter so she could pursue a formal education instead of following her family's chosen path. She often volunteers for us. Her connection to Erin is entirely coincidental."

There was that word again.

"Where is the rest of her tribe now?"

Isaac blanched and then asked quietly, "You're the one who killed them?"

"Then they are—were—hunters?"

Isaac nodded slowly. "But Marissa chose not to follow that path. She is no threat to you."

Adjila knew that Isaac was telling the truth, but he suspected there was more to the story. He would get it later, probably from Marissa herself.

"Nice chatting with you," he said before pushing his way past the security doors.

"Wait!"

"Go away while I'm still in a good mood," Adjila commanded. At the same time, he reached out for the minds of the nurses and doctors who had jumped when he'd trespassed on their domain. Each fell asleep instantly, and Adjila continued freely toward the patients' rooms.

He identified Erin's room immediately by the young shapeshifter guarding the doorway. Sassy's blue gaze was piercing, and unlike Isaac, he showed no outward signs of fear.

Either Shevaun's "puppy" had a death wish, or he was very good at keeping himself under control. Adjila suspected the latter. It was a necessary survival skill for a Pakana who had neither been raised by Pack nor chosen to join one later.

"If you don't make a fuss, I'll let you come with us,"

Adjila offered. "If you decide to make trouble, I'll leave you behind."

"Are you going to hurt Erin?" Sassy asked, a hint of a tremor in his voice now as he said his friend's name.

"I am going to do whatever I must to fix this mess and protect Shevaun," Adjila answered honestly, "but I don't plan to hurt Erin unless it is required."

Sassy nodded, seeming to accept that as the most he would get.

Adjila turned away from the hyena, wondering about his response. He didn't plan to hurt Erin because that might pose a risk to Shevaun, but the truth was he simply didn't *want* to hurt her, either.

Shevaun's strange melancholy was affecting him; that was all.

The girl was sleeping when he stepped into the room, but it wasn't a peaceful sleep. Occasionally she uttered a word or a phrase in Latin. He listened for a minute before he realized she had to be dreaming about Shevaun's last night as a human.

He touched her forehead and pushed her deeper into sleep, where dreams would not bother her.

"Follow me," he said to Sassy as he lifted the sleeping girl in his arms. "Do you know where they would keep the rest of her records?" He doubted that the hospital had given everything to SingleEarth's doctor, unless Erin had already agreed to go with him. Hospitals had a tendency to limit the amount of information they gave to strangers.

"They should have copies in the office," Sassy answered. "The head nurse . . ." He hesitated as he moved into the front hall and saw the people Adjila had left sleeping there. He looked up as if he was about to object, and then just shook his head and grabbed a key card from one of the unconscious nurses. "I'll get them."

The shapeshifter was as good as his word. He found Erin's records in the file cabinet and then printed something out from the computer.

"I might have manipulated you before, but I meant what I said about Erin's medications," he said as he proffered the printout. "This is the list of what she's on at the moment. If she suddenly stops taking all of them, it could go very badly for her."

"I need to get rid of the drugs in her system before I can do much with her," Adjila said. "I'll be sure to keep an eye on her physical condition while I do so."

The boy nodded.

"Come along," Adjila said as he led the way back down to the car, with Erin still asleep in his arms.

Chapter 18

SHEVAUN THREW ASIDE THE CANVAS, which cracked against the wall. She had brought her paints and brushes from France, but they were betraying her just like her mind.

For her first attempt, she had laid a base coat of paint in shades of green, beige, and brown over one of the silk-screened "paintings" that were hanging in this otherwise attractive colonial-style house. She could see a dense forest in her mind's eye, but she almost gave up before she finished covering the ugly flowery meadow already on the canvas.

She managed only to streak the next canvas in gold and red before she realized she was painting the inside of a church. She threw that one across the room, splattering linseed oil and pigment on the couch and what was probably a handmade lace blanket.

For her next attempt, she didn't bother trying to obscure the original image—a sunset and a white chapel—but sketched over it, using her paintbrush like a stick of charcoal. Eventually, she had to step back, because she realized she didn't even know what she was trying to paint.

She tilted her head, looking at the black and gray lines.

It was a sword fight. One man was on the ground, and another had just been run through. A third man, standing, looked at the scene with horror.

O, I am fortune's fool!

She recognized the scene at last, from *Romeo and Juliet*. She had no idea why she had painted it.

This time she flung not only the canvas, but the brushes and paint thinner and pigment, too, in one violent motion. Painting normally calmed and focused her, but this time, she didn't even feel in control of her hands—or the rest of her body. Of all the silly things, she kept finding herself *breathing*. She noticed because the fumes let off by the oils were intense; normally they didn't affect her, even in closed-off rooms like this, because she didn't need air.

"Shevaun?" Iana peered around the corner and into the room.

"I thought you went hunting," Shevaun said.

"Brittany did," Iana said. "I didn't want to leave you alone."

Shevaun put her hands against the wall and dropped her head, taking another deep breath of pungent air.

"I'm fine," she said. She had to pull herself together, for Brittany's and Iana's sakes, if not for her own.

Iana began going about the room, picking up the strewn brushes and swirling them in a tin of turpentine so that the paint wouldn't harden and destroy them. Shevaun had once tried to teach the girls to paint. They had been curious because Shevaun enjoyed it, but neither turned out to have much passion for the art.

"I'm fine," she said again, fighting the instinct to breathe once more after she voiced those words.

She jumped when the door opened. Smiled when she saw the hyena. Frowned when she realized she was smiling at him. And then her eyes widened as Adjila followed with Erin cradled unconscious in his arms.

She moved forward, and Sassy stepped quickly out of the way.

"I'm not sure that's a good idea," Adjila said as Shevaun started to lift her hand to touch the girl's cheek.

It took a conscious effort for Shevaun to drop her hand. She was about to take a step back when the girl's eyes fluttered open. They were a brownish shade of hazel, muddy green, and so dilated that even the faint light in the room had to be blinding to her.

Despite that, somehow Erin's eyes focused. Those wide pupils, which nearly obliterated the irises, now seemed as black as a vampire's eyes. They became prismatic, and then they became mirrors, in which Shevaun felt like she could see herself, not only as she was in that moment, but as she could have been in a thousand different lives. . . .

If she had turned down Theron's offer of immortality, she could have become the wife of one of the invaders, as many of her kin and friends had. She might have had a glorious life, with natural children born to her. Grandchildren. Perhaps distant heirs still alive today, instead of just *her.*

She could see herself as a child, if she were still mortal in this modern day. She could feel the pulse in her temples, even though her heart hadn't beat for centuries, and the stench of turpentine and linseed oil was overpowering enough to make her head spin.

"No," she whispered.

"Shevaun?" The concerned inquiry from Iana seemed distant.

She felt as if she were drowning, or suffocating.

Erin let out a cry as Shevaun pulled her from Adjila's arms, planning to . . . she didn't even know what. Snap the girl's neck, probably. The instant they touched, though, Shevaun's world warped. One moment she was looking into Erin's eyes—and the next, she was looking *through* them.

The clash of thoughts in Shevaun's mind was deafening as a thousand voices talked simultaneously. Everything was spinning, until at last she shrieked and flung the girl across the room with the last of her energy.

Shevaun heard a crack as fragile human bones hit the wall with deadly force.

She felt Erin's bones break, as if they were her own, and she screamed. She had suffered plenty of injuries in her life, but vampires couldn't feel pain at the same level that humans did, and Erin's body seemed to be crying, *We're broken, badly. We need help or we will die.*

Shevaun had to get away.

She fled, dashing through the door as Adjila shouted, "Iana, go after her!"

She ran faster.

"Shevaun, please!"

She had to do . . . something. . . . She didn't know what, just that if she couldn't act, immediately, she would simply go mad—if she hadn't already. What was *wrong* with her?

The tigers. That was how this had all started. She knew where one of them was.

Classes were out, but Marissa—quite possibly the last surviving member of her tribe—was still at school. She was sitting next to her car in the school parking lot, leaning over a book and butchering the French language. Shevaun watched Marissa for a few moments before the tiger let out a guttural cry and flung the book from her; it narrowly missed another car's rearview mirror as it fluttered open and landed on the concrete.

Marissa dropped her head to her knees and struggled to repress a sob.

Shevaun had meant to pounce so swiftly the girl wouldn't even have a chance to cry out, but something in that sob pierced her, and she found herself walking across the parking lot slowly, weaving between cars but finally letting herself come into the tiger's line of sight well before she reached her.

Marissa looked up with tear-rimmed eyes, but the expression on her face was mostly just . . . *blank.*

"Have you come to kill me?" she asked flatly. She reached to her back and drew one of the slender blades favored by hunters. For a moment Shevaun thought Marissa planned to try to fight, but instead, Marissa threw the knife so that it clattered to a stop at Shevaun's feet. "Go ahead. If you need more blood to satisfy you, it might as well be mine, right? This whole thing is my fault, anyway."

Again, Shevaun's intention of violence was pushed aside, this time by a wave of guilt and . . . affection? She shook her head, trying to clear it of what she knew had to be lingering emotions from Erin's mind, but it did no good.

She knelt beside Marissa, who flinched but didn't try to run.

"I'm sorry," Shevaun said, though she didn't know why.

"My family tried to kill you," Marissa answered. "What else could you do in response?" She bowed her head again. "Is Erin still alive?"

Shevaun had to bite back a growl at the girl's name. Instead of answering, she asked, "Your fault—how?" Had this girl meddled with Erin somehow, maybe even tried to heal her friend, and caused the mess Shevaun was now in?

"Someone told me about Erin a few weeks ago. That she wasn't just crazy. They sent me her medical records, and your name was mentioned a lot, with enough details that I knew it had to actually be . . . *you.* I knew that most of my family were hunters, and it scared me to realize that the girl I was getting to know was mixed up with someone as dangerous as you. I should have told SingleEarth about her so they could have helped her. Instead, I asked my family what they thought I should do." She swallowed tightly. "They told me to watch her. See who else she associated with. See if she could fight. And they told me they would deal with it."

So there had been a reason the tigers had gone after Shevaun in France: to protect their kin. They had probably hired the human hunters to help because they knew they were going after a quarry beyond their skills, which they would never have targeted otherwise.

Shevaun would have done the same.

She *had* done the same, many times.

How could she possibly blame them?

She stood, pressing a hand to her chest as if she expected to feel her heart pounding. She didn't want to talk to the tiger anymore or have any more questions answered. She disliked the answers she had already enough.

"Erin is alive," she said. "She'll stay alive if . . ." If what? "If we can save her without sacrificing my family."

"And me?" Marissa asked softly.

"We've done you enough damage."

Shevaun turned away, tasting her own blood as she bit her lip to keep from crying. She wasn't supposed to feel this way. She had to fix things. Maybe once Adjila severed the connection to Erin, this pain would pass, again leaving her feeling free . . . but maybe it wouldn't. Maybe it wasn't *supposed* to. Seeking absolution, she fled once more, to a place that had long ago offered her solace.

Chapter 19

"YOU'RE GOING TO BE FINE," Erin could hear someone saying. "You're going to be—She *is* going to be fine, *right?*"

"Yes, she'll be fine. *Back off!*"

Searing pain shot up and down Erin's spine, reminding her that she had a body and was confined to it . . . but why did she need reminding of that? *And why did it have to be true?*

"Thank you, for helping her. I know you would probably rather—"

"The girls went for Shevaun." That was Adjila, speaking in quick, terse sentences. "Distance from Erin is probably a good thing for her right now anyway. I can't help Shevaun unless I can heal Erin and shut down this damn *link.*"

"You're going to be fine," the first voice said again, and this time she recognized it. Sassy.

Erin followed the conversation only peripherally. She

couldn't seem to open her eyes. She wanted to scream, as if the air might expel with itself some of the pain, but she couldn't even whimper, because she couldn't draw a deep enough breath.

"Calm down," Adjila snapped. "Erin, stop doing whatever you're doing."

"Whatever she's doing, I doubt it's intentional," Sassy replied. The words should have been sharp, but he spoke them in the same calm, reassuring tone he had used before, probably for her benefit.

Erin wanted to ask *What happened?* but at that moment, another shock of pain went through her. This time she did cry out, even though doing so felt like it constricted her lungs impossibly.

"How badly is she hurt?" Sassy asked.

"Well, she obviously has some less than human blood in her, or she would have been dead on impact," Adjila answered. The blunt words fell on Erin's ears like quills, hooking into her. Fortunately, the phrase "less than human" caught first, leaving little room for the fear of death. "If she were with human doctors, she would surely die, but once I get past the drugs in her system, she should be fine."

Less than human.

Was she hallucinating?

Hallucinations didn't hurt this much.

She was grateful when everything turned gray. The world went quiet and the pain faded to a low background roar like the sound of pounding surf.

*　*　*

Was she in a *church?* Erin couldn't remember the last time she had been in one. She hadn't been raised to be particularly religious. Even if she had been, years of trying to understand and identify basic, daily reality hadn't made her anxious to try to explore the unseen world and question the possibility of divinity.

She wasn't just in a church, she realized. She was wearing some kind of tunic-like dress made of red brocade.

This has to be a dream.

Looking around, she realized that the elaborate stained-glass windows and gold-touched frescoes depicted abstract instead of religious scenes. It was as if someone had taken a watercolor of a church and soaked it until all the colors had run.

When Erin walked forward now, her footsteps splashed, making the stone floor ripple.

"Hello?"

"Why won't you leave me *alone?*" The cry came from the opposite side of the building. With the whole world melting around her, Erin moved toward the voice and found Shevaun.

"I came here to be alone," Shevaun said. "*You* aren't supposed to come past the gate."

"I'm sorry," Erin replied.

She turned to go, but the walls and doors had melted together. Bits of glass from the windows crunched beneath her feet and then dissolved into puddles of color. She turned back to Shevaun.

"Why am I seeing you?" Erin asked. "I never see you in my dreams. I usually *am* you."

"I dream about this place sometimes," Shevaun replied. "Vampires aren't supposed to be able to dream at all, but I've done it a lot lately. Maybe I have you to thank for that. Or curse for it."

She looked up, and Erin followed her gaze. The ceiling had melted away, and above them, the moon was full. Looking at it made Erin's skin crawl. She heard a yipping, chattering bark in the distance.

The sound made Shevaun frown. "Stop that! You're messing everything up!"

The full moon outside the window began to darken as it was devoured by an eclipse.

"*I'm* messing everything up?" Erin shouted back. "*You* have ruined the last eight years of my life! Why won't you just *go away*?" She stalked toward Shevaun but stopped when she saw the body on the floor, half in and half out of it. "That has to be from your mind," she said, unnerved. She didn't have enough experience with mangled corpses to imagine them this vividly on her own.

Just a dream, she told herself. *Dreams can't hurt you. They might be able to help you learn about your alter, if you don't freak out like last time.*

"They're all mine," Shevaun answered, looking around. The walls and windows and pews and floor were covered in bodies now. They all had their eyes open and were gaz-ing blindly toward Shevaun.

Never mind learning and psychotherapy, Erin thought. *If this turns into a zombie dream, I am going to scream until I wake up.*

"I want you out of my head," Erin said.

"Something we agree on," Shevaun replied. "There was a reason I let Theron change me. I didn't like being mor-tal. I don't like feeling like one again. So . . . shoo! Go! Leave me be!"

Erin stepped back and narrowly avoided tripping on one of the bodies. "This is *my* crazy brain. You don't exist. So *you* shoo!"

"Maybe I'm the one who's crazy and you're the one who doesn't exist," Shevaun replied, with her own fine logic. "I would be quite happy with your not existing, but I fear you actually *do*, outside my mind. I wonder, though . . ." She stood, her brocade tunic not even wrinkled. "If I killed you here, would you snap back into your own body, or would you just snap . . . out?"

This dream was starting to seem a little more intimi-dating. *What* would *happen if we fought here?* Erin wondered. Could Shevaun be right? Could Erin be destroyed in this dreamscape?

Don't panic. You're real, she's *just a fantasy.*

"Even if I'm only a figment of your imagination, right now I exist at least as much as you do," Shevaun replied, as if in response to Erin's thoughts. She walked forward, her movements slick like a hunting cat's. "I think I—"

"Erin, can you hear me? You have to come back now."

* * *

The church faded away, and Erin suddenly found herself back in what she thought had to be the real world, except that Adjila was talking to her. But that was silly, since Adjila didn't exist. Even if he had saved her life somehow. *Less than human.* Was she still dreaming?

She tried to remember what had happened. She had been at the hospital. The SingleEarth doctor had spoken to her, and then Marissa had, and then Tina. Their discussion had seemed to disturb the psychologist, no matter how hard Tina had tried to conceal it. She had insisted that Erin had only gone missing a handful of times over the years, and even then it had never been for more than a few hours.

In other words, Shevaun and a stranger named Adjila could never have met and formed a relationship.

So what was he doing here now?

Erin tried not to think about that and instead tried to remember the events at the hospital.

The conversation with Tina had upset her. The hospital had given her something for the anxiety that was stronger than the medicine she normally took. By the time Sassy had arrived, she had been woozy and incoherent. She remembered asking him to stay until she woke up.

It felt safer that way.

When she *had* woken, she had noticed Sassy standing nearby, but only briefly before her attention had gone to Shevaun. This time she was not an image in the mirror, but an actual person walking toward her. Shevaun had touched Erin's arm, and then the world had gone to hell. For the first time, Erin had *felt* her own alter ego surge to the forefront.

No, alter egos. It was as if her mind had been turned into a kaleidoscope and she had looked at the world through a hundred subtly different views.

And then that world had exploded in pain, and the Shevauns inside her head had screamed and tried to flee the damaged flesh, trampling Erin in their path before everything went dark.

"Erin, wake up," Sassy said when Erin refused to respond to Adjila's voice. "You're okay now."

She tried and managed to open her eyes. That was when she realized she was in an unfamiliar kitchen, lying on her stomach on the table, with Sassy holding one of her hands.

"I am so not 'okay' now," she whispered, closing her eyes again.

"She should be stable," Adjila said. He glanced out the window, where it appeared to be either dawn or dusk; Erin wasn't sure which. "I need to get to Shevaun and the girls. You two . . . come with me."

"Sassy, would you confirm for me that the imaginary person is talking to us?" Erin asked, still refusing to open her eyes, as if not looking would help her hold on to her precarious understanding of what was real in the world.

"I'll explain it all in a minute," Sassy answered. "First I think we should do what the cranky, impatient witch wants."

Cranky and impatient described the expression on

Adjila's face well, Erin decided, after she forced herself to look at him. She rolled over and sat up, feeling an odd twinge down her back, but nothing as bad as she would have expected based on the earlier pain.

"I was hurt," she said, trying to piece together those jumbled memories.

Sassy nodded and bit his lip. Adjila, who was leading them through a disheveled, paint-strewn living room, paused to glance at the far wall.

Erin followed his gaze and found a body-sized indent in the plaster, accompanied by a cracked beam. The dark swatches of color on it were unmistakably blood.

"Most of your spine was crushed," Adjila explained as she continued to stare, "and your skull was broken. That's not to mention the lesser injuries, such as a broken scapula and several punctured or ruptured organs, including both of your lungs."

Erin swayed on her feet. Sassy supported her as she walked, dazed, toward the spot, which should have been the site of her demise.

"How?" she managed to choke out.

"Shevaun's kind is exceptionally strong, and she was very frightened and very angry," Adjila answered. "You are lucky that *my* kind is good at healing, when we choose to do so."

He pulled open what appeared to be a cellar door, and gestured for them to proceed. Erin hesitated, still staring over her shoulder at the living room, but Sassy pulled her forward.

"Why are we letting the should-be-imaginary ... witch ... lock us up?" Erin asked as Adjila shut the door behind them. She heard the *snick* of a bolt lock sliding into place.

Witch. She had said it. She wasn't sure yet that she believed it, but if she believed *anything* that had happened that day, it would have to include the fact that Adjila existed, because otherwise she would be dead.

"Because ..." Sassy hesitated, and she heard him fumbling against the walls, probably looking for a light switch. "Because we couldn't stop him if we tried. Because I don't want to make a pest of myself and be taken away from you. And because if we don't piss him off, I think he can help you. Even if his ultimate goal is to help Shevaun, he needs to keep you safe and fix whatever's wrong with you to do that."

"What if killing me is what it takes to help her?" Erin asked.

She blinked as Sassy found a lamp and the sudden glare assaulted her. For an instant, Sassy was haloed against the light, giving him a strange angelic aura.

"Then I'll fight for you," Sassy answered. "But if they want us dead ... well ..." He shrugged.

Erin took a deep breath as she looked around what appeared to be a semifinished basement apartment. The walls were bare and the carpeting was ripped up as if someone had been in the process of removing it; a bucket of plaster stood open on the floor, its contents hardened and cracked, as if whoever had been working had been pulled away suddenly.

Looking at the tools, she could almost remember her own fair hands pulling the young worker close, and her own teeth piercing his throat, as she prepared to occupy this house for as long as it took to fix the problem of a girl named Erin.

Chapter 20

ADJILA STEPPED WEARILY over the church's threshold, resisting the urge to watch the gold-backed portraits above the doorway. What the devil was Shevaun doing here?

Shevaun held no fondness for religion, but sacrilege did not appeal to her, either. He could count the times she had willingly stepped into God's house over the hundreds of years they had been together. She would even give up chasing her prey should they cross onto holy ground, though vampires certainly had no innate problems with such things. With the moonlight shining on her hair, which had darkened over the centuries, she would laugh and say, "I don't think I'm welcome."

He wouldn't have believed that Shevaun was here, except that he could feel her. He knew the flavor of her power, and even now that it was twisted, infected with that human girl's, he could still recognize it as well as he could recognize the fear on Iana's and Brittany's faces as they waited for him in the entryway. Brittany had been the one to get him from the house, while Iana had stayed to keep an eye on Shevaun. Neither dared to move past the royal doors and into the main church area, where nonbelievers were not supposed to tread.

That, too, was a tradition Shevaun had always respected. Adjila disregarded this now; Shevaun's safety held a higher priority in his mind than her religious beliefs. He did not fail to note, however, that the denomination of this particular church—Eastern Orthodox—was the closest modern equivalent to the church in which Shevaun had been raised.

If she feared the memories and sensations of humanity that her tie to Erin brought, then perhaps it made sense that she would turn to the one place that had brought her comfort the last time she had experienced those emotions.

Perhaps.

As Brittany and Iana left to go home, Adjila moved past the royal doors, and he finally caught sight of Shevaun. His heart sped for just an instant before he forced it to calm. Control over his physical form was one of the first skills Pandora had taught him, after all.

Shevaun did not notice him. She did not look up as Adjila approached and knelt beside her; she didn't react to him at all.

"Shevaun?" He started to reach out but didn't want to touch her until he had her attention, since she could react suddenly and violently if startled.

She completely failed to respond to his voice.

He paused to examine her condition more closely and assure himself that she was not injured. Blood was smeared on her hands, arms, and face, and in her hair, but none of it was hers. She must have gone hunting. The blood was an addition to the swatches of paint that had already been on her skin.

He had often seen her coated in blood or streaked with paint or charcoal, but she had always cleaned herself afterward. He had never seen her this filthy, with her hair matted and the blood congealing.

"Shevaun?" he said, a little more anxiously, as he tentatively reached out to touch her, hoping not to lose an arm.

She had been fine before he brought Erin home. *Fine*. A little moody maybe, but with Shevaun, that was a relative term. Sometimes she got moody for no reason he could detect; sometimes she explained it to him, and sometimes she kept her thoughts to herself. That was the way it had been for centuries. Her moods and whims meant the difference between a new painting and a bloody swath through Europe.

What she *never* did was disappear. Even during her most artistic, eccentric rampages, Shevaun was loyal to a fault. But she had stormed out after seeing Erin nearly thirty-six hours earlier, and had lost Iana quickly. It had taken Adjila until twilight to heal Erin, and it was now almost time for another sunset.

"Shevaun, we need to get you home," he said, slowly pulling her toward him. He expected her to be tense, but she relaxed in his arms and let him hold her. "Brittany and

Iana are waiting there," he added, to no avail. "Erin is too." Nothing. "With Sassy." She tightened her grip on him, but he didn't know if her response had anything to do with the names he had spoken.

He smiled darkly, imagining the expression she would wear when this was all over. She might have been born in the fifteenth century, but Shevaun had been liberated and independent before the concept of women's suffrage. It was going to stick in her craw that she ended up a damsel in such distress that someone else had to take care of her.

Getting her home was . . . interesting. People in the city of Boston noticed when a man walked by carrying a catatonic woman, so it was a good thing Adjila was well practiced at quelling such reactions. As he carried Shevaun to the car, he sent out gentle thoughts like a wave: *Nothing to see, nothing to remember.*

The instant he stepped into the house they had "borrowed" for their stay in Massachusetts, Brittany and Iana ran to greet him, asking the same questions that had drummed through his mind: "Is she all right? What is going *on*? Can you fix it?"

Brittany took a single glance at Shevaun's condition and instantly asked, "Who do I kill?"

"Whoever it is, you'll have to fight me for him," Adjila replied. He no longer feared the potential wrath of the witch who might have a claim on Erin. Now he wanted a chance to put his hands on the throat of whoever was responsible for this travesty.

He set Shevaun down gently on the couch, one of the

few pieces of furniture in the living room that had sur-vived her rampage, and then knelt beside her, one hand over hers and the other over her heart. Trusting the girls to keep watch—and given their current mood, slaughter anyone who dared to intrude—he tried to find Shevaun, who seemed to be lost somewhere inside her own thoughts.

What have they done to you, my beautiful whirlwind? he thought as he struggled to move past conflicting images, some from her mind and some from Erin's.

After a few failed attempts, he turned to Brittany and Iana, who were pacing behind him, and said, "Why don't you two go hunt?"

"I already fed," Brittany replied.

More firmly, Adjila said, "Go hunt *something*. It will help you calm down, and it will help me examine Shevaun."

As soon as he said it was for Shevaun's own good, the girls exchanged a look. "Come on," Iana said to her sister, and then they both left him alone.

The peace didn't last long, though; he had barely had a chance to direct his attention back to Shevaun when knocking interrupted his concentration. He stood with a frown and had taken two steps toward the front door when he realized that the sound had of course come from the cellar, where Erin and Sassy had been locked for about twenty-four hours. At least there was a bathroom down there.

He might have ignored them—humans could live a long

time without food, and there was water available to them from the sink—but that he had taken even a second to locate the sound meant he was too tired and distracted to be messing around with Shevaun's mind. He needed a break.

He opened the door cautiously, wondering if the hyena puppy had come up with some ill-thought-out escape plan.

Sassy was indeed standing by the door, but he didn't look about to bolt. He glanced at the bottom of the stairs, where Erin was waiting, before he said, "It's nearly night. Also, we haven't eaten all day. Any chance you plan on dealing with either of these problems?"

"There's some food in the kitchen. Help yourself." When Erin took a tentative step toward the stairs, Adjila added, "Erin, you can wait down there."

"We aren't going to run," Sassy said. "You don't need to hold her hostage."

Adjila shook his head. "I know you're not going to run. I want to make sure I have the link between Erin and Shevaun sealed off completely before they're in the same room again."

Sassy waited for Erin to nod in agreement before leaving her behind.

Adjila watched the shapeshifter cross the living room toward the kitchen, Sassy's emotions as carefully controlled as his movements. The power swirling around Sassy was thicker now, tight with tension. Looking at it made Adjila realize he had misunderstood what the boy had said a minute ago. He hadn't said, "It's nearly night and I haven't eaten all day." The two issues were barely even related.

It was nearly night; more importantly, the full moon was just becoming visible. The willpower that had kept the boy rational so far was impressive, but Adjila doubted it would last forever. If the Pakana wasn't outside in the moonlight where he could shift and stretch his other form, soon he would become dangerous to himself and anyone around him—including, quite possibly, his dear Erin.

Maybe it's time I took a student, Adjila found himself thinking, only to shake his head.

He had to concentrate on the situation at hand: safeguarding Shevaun's power from external influences—like Erin's mind. Then he could see if Erin or Sassy had anything to contribute that would help solve this mystery.

If Shevaun were hurt in the process . . . well, Adjila would go to his own grave before he would let her go to hers.

Chapter 21

ERIN'S STOMACH GRUMBLED as she paced, careful not to trip over the shreds of carpet in the unfinished basement. There were no windows down here, and so no natural light. Sassy had said it was a little before sunset, but she wasn't sure she believed that—or any of the things he had told her.

What she did know for sure was that she had been locked in this beneath-ground apartment long enough to miss a full day's worth of all her medications. Her father *would* have called the police this time. He would be frantic looking for her.

She hadn't been able to sleep, and the hours of insomnia had taken their toll. She was distracted by the slow seep of colors into her vision and the soft murmur of voices that weren't there. She had lost time—usually just seconds or minutes—in the middle of conversations and knew that Sassy had noticed.

It would surely get worse, and quickly.

Finally, she sat on one of the rolls of carpet and waited.

"You keep this place pretty well stocked," she heard Sassy say upstairs.

"The owners left it that way," Adjila replied. He sounded tired. "How long are you safe for?"

Sassy hesitated, his steps slowing. "Until sundown at least. Maybe longer. I haven't tested my control in a while. Hey—" He paused. "This is Erin's, isn't it?"

"Mhmm." Adjila sounded distracted now. "Tell Erin to join us. I think I've stabilized Shevaun enough to keep her from connecting with Erin for the time being, as long as they don't touch again."

Erin was already halfway up the stairs when Sassy appeared in the open doorway with something tucked under his arm. "He says it's all right," he said.

"I heard." She looked warily at where Shevaun lay on the couch, apparently asleep. "I would feel safer if she were at least in another room. Or preferably back in France."

"Your sense of safety doesn't concern me," Adjila responded, "and I don't want her out of my sight. With your cooperation, maybe we can figure out how this all happened before Brittany and Iana get back and try to eat you."

Erin balked. Sassy had told her that the women were vampires. Stranger than that, when she had "dreamed" about being in Sète she actually *had* been there, albeit in Shevaun's body. But she was still having trouble wrapping her head around it all.

Now Sassy pulled Erin's attention back to the present by handing her a photo album. "I think this is yours," he said. "Though I have no idea why it's here."

Still feeling more than a little dazed, Erin sat down at the kitchen table. Sassy had found milk, cookies, a jar of honey-roasted peanuts, a box of oranges, and an assortment of granola bars, all of which were spread out across the table.

Erin started to reach for a granola bar, but her stomach rolled in a way that was decidedly *not* hunger-related, and she changed her mind.

"It's here because Shevaun found it when she searched your house," Adjila said bluntly. "It had a strong effect on her, but I assume any 'power' it contains is sentimental."

Erin nodded. Her two favorites were the one at the end of the album—a shot of her and her father in front of the Boston Opera House, when they had seen a musical to celebrate her having gone a year without hospitalization— and the one at the very front, which was the only picture of her mother she had.

Erin looked up from the album to Adjila, who shouldn't exist, to Sassy, the pathological liar, and then to Shevaun, her alter ego, very clearly sleeping on the couch in the next room. This was crazy. It was *absurd.*

And yet it felt real. Completely, utterly *real.*

"Why is she unconscious but I'm not?" she asked. Not that she wanted Shevaun awake, but she did want to understand . . . something, anything.

"Because you may know something that can help,"

Adjila answered, "and because if you go mad, you're easier to control than Shevaun is. I'm hard to kill, but she could do it if she tried."

"What—" She fought to suppress a sob, or was it a giggle? She was on the verge of hysteria and she knew it. She couldn't even look at Adjila without feeling even more crazy, because the seductive thoughts running through her head were obviously Shevaun's. "What could I possibly know?"

"I'll start with what I know," Adjila said. "I know you have someone else's magic on you. Someone, somewhere along the line, meddled with your mind and your magic."

"You have got to be kidding me," she said.

"Even humans have some level of power," Adjila replied patiently. "Shapeshifters, like your friend Sassy there, have more. Individuals like Shevaun and me have even more, as well as an advanced ability to control that power. At the most basic level, that power is what makes you alive and self-aware. It's what keeps your skin in place or, in the case of a shapeshifter, allows that skin to slip into a new form. More importantly, it's what keeps your thoughts contained and keeps the rest of the world out of your head. But your power is broken."

"That can't be good," she said, and couldn't suppress a manic giggle. "What's that mean?"

Adjila glared at her, and Sassy took her hand and squeezed it.

"It means you have no protection or control over whatever your natural power should be," Adjila said.

"Which means . . . ?"

"It means . . ." He drew a deep breath. "It means your mind isn't protected, so you're likely to hear thoughts that others project. You're likely to see or feel power, constantly, since the part of you that should block that out just doesn't work. And it means you have a large, gaping hole in your defenses, which is matched by some kind of strange connection to Shevaun. So instead of just having your own memories, you have hers as well. When something triggers her personality, her memories take control. Shevaun is more equipped to defend you from danger, after all, than you are."

"But it wasn't just Erin's memories that were in France with you," Sassy interjected. "Erin *remembers* being there herself."

"Shevaun was hurt," Adjila said. "I had to suppress her power. I didn't know about the link to Erin, so I didn't guard against it, and I left her vulnerable."

Sassy smirked. "So what you're saying is, this is all *your* fault?"

Adjila glared. Before he could retort, though, Erin asked with a slightly raised voice, "Does stuff like this go wrong a lot, or is it just me? If it's just me, do you know *how* it happened? Or why?"

Can you fix me?

She was too scared to ask that last question, though.

"I don't know yet how it happened," Adjila said. "You may naturally have had psychic ability that was damaged by some kind of injury, maybe an accident. That wouldn't explain your link to Shevaun specifically, but it would explain the damage to your power that allowed the link to form."

Erin swallowed tightly, recalling what the doctor from SingleEarth had told her. "My mother was injured in an accident and I had to be delivered prematurely. I nearly died. I stopped breathing more than once."

She opened the photo album as she spoke, so that she could look at the photograph of the woman who had lost her life giving Erin hers.

"That certainly could have done it," Adjila answered thoughtfully. "That level of trauma at birth can trigger psychic ability even in humans *not* genetically predisposed to it, and we already know you are—"

"Don't say it again," Erin said, cringing. *A little more or less than human,* she knew.

"Okay," Adjila replied, his tone still scientific and controlled. "Do you know how your mother was injured? I don't supposed it matters, but—"

He broke off abruptly. When Erin looked up, she realized he was staring at the photograph of her mother. His face had paled, as if he were viewing a ghost.

Chapter 22

"WHAT?" ERIN ASKED when Adjila finally ripped his gaze away from the photograph.

"There is something you have to understand about Shevaun," he said. He walked to the doorway between the two rooms and stood there a moment, looking at the unconscious vampire. "She is as beautiful and merciless a hunter as ever roamed this earth. I have seen her lay waste an entire village, and bring an empire to its knees. They say Nero played the fiddle when Rome burned. Well, I have seen Shevaun paint in the sunset of a—"

"Can you get to the point?" Sassy interrupted with a growl.

Erin was prepared to shush him, but when she looked at him, his normally blue eyes had become dark brown and seemed to shine, reflecting the overhead light.

She swallowed tightly.

"Sorry," he said, dropping his gaze. "Adjila, you were saying?"

"My *point*," Adjila said, "is that Shevaun is one of the fiercest women I have ever known, but she isn't *cold*. She still loves, and she still has things that she cherishes. And while she can kill mercilessly when she wishes to, she chooses her prey with compassion, and she does not kill *accidentally*."

Adjila still hadn't turned back to look at them. Erin couldn't even see his face. Even so, there was something about his posture that made her sure the emotion he was hiding was shame. Some part of her could read him, in the same way she could speak both ancient and modern languages, and knew how to mix oils without ever having done it, and knew history she hadn't studied but seemed to have lived through. It was the part of her brain that knew the great works of literature and the location of every vital organ in the human body but had never learned the modern details of atomic theory or chemistry.

Erin shuddered, understanding now that this knowledge was not hers alone but came from the memories of a centuries-old vampire.

"Sixteen years ago," Adjila said, "we were attacked. We run into hunters often enough, but these were higher-caliber hunters than normal. Shevaun took two poisoned bolts, one to the stomach and one to the throat. I was hit, too, which is why it took me time to get to her side. Shevaun grabbed the nearest mortal she could find to feed and thus heal." He paused there, one hand gripping the doorframe, his gaze still pointedly averted from Erin and Sassy.

Erin didn't need Shevaun's knowledge to realize suddenly where this story was going. She noticed she was holding her breath, and forced herself to draw air into her lungs. She knew what he was about to say, but he couldn't be saying . . . he *couldn't* be.

"It was an emergency," Adjila said. "Neither of us was paying attention."

He turned back toward the kitchen, and once Erin could see Shevaun again, the vampire's memory came to her as vividly as one of her own.

The bolts had firestone in them. It wasn't powerful enough to kill Shevaun immediately, but she knew she needed blood quickly to stop it from doing more damage while Adjila healed her.

Moments earlier, the streets had been crowded, but most of the humans had panicked and fled when the bolts had flown into the crowd from the shadows. One woman had fallen, and leaned against the side of a building, wide-eyed and smelling like power. She had shapeshifter blood. That was good.

Normally Shevaun hesitated to kill an innocent who just happened to be in the wrong place at the wrong time, but her own survival came first. Shevaun reached for the woman, and as she started to heal and the pain began to fade, she listened to the woman's heartbeat.

Thump-thump. Thum-thum-thump-thump. What . . .

Shevaun drew back, despite her still-burning hunger, and finally looked *at the woman she had caught. The woman with two heartbeats. The woman whose loose day dress had hidden at first glance her bulging stomach.*

Both heartbeats stopped.

No . . . no . . . Shevaun lifted her head.

"Adjila!"

"I think this is the reason she still avoids churches, for fear of God's rejection, and calls Brittany and Iana her daughters," Adjila explained. "When she started screaming that day, she begged me to undo what she had done. I can heal many things, but when a human is stripped of power, it isn't just a matter of physical injury. The body simply *stops.* There's nothing subtle about it, and all I could think to do was shove power at both the mother and the child to keep them alive long enough for human doctors to arrive and take them off our hands.

"And, frankly, I didn't give it another thought— until now."

"Wow," Sassy responded, "you screwed up pretty badly there, didn'tcha?"

Adjila turned with a glare, and Erin tensed in expectation of his anger, but then he shut his eyes and spoke calmly.

"If it's just my power tying the two of you, I should be able to break the bond. Once that link is gone, Shevaun should be safe."

"And me?" Erin asked. If she had understood Adjila, then the bond to Shevaun was a secondary problem, beyond the damage caused by—

She killed my mother.

The knowledge had taken several seconds to process, but now it hit her like a fist to the stomach.

"I will help you learn to control whatever power or abilities you have left," Adjila answered. "After I break the bond to Shevaun, I'll call Pandora—my teacher— and ask for her help. It's easier to break a mind than fix it, after all."

"Why would you help us?" Sassy asked. "Once Shevaun's safe, why wouldn't you just dump us back in the hospital?"

"If nothing else," Adjila replied, "my kind believes in cleaning up our own mistakes. Besides, I think Pandora will be curious about such an unusual, accidental scenario." He looked at Sassy intently, as if evaluating him. "I think she will be interested in you, as well."

"What does *that* mean?"

Erin could hardly even hear what Adjila and Sassy were saying anymore, knowing she was standing just one room away from the woman who had stolen her mother's life— to protect her own. Erin had Shevaun's memories and knew not only the pain and desperation that had led her to reach for the nearest living soul to feed and heal, but also felt the horror and guilt that Shevaun had experienced when she realized what she had done.

Erin wanted to be able to hate the woman who had

done this to her, but that wouldn't be necessary. Shevaun already hated herself enough for that moment.

"Let's get on with this, then," she said. She wanted to be rid of this link with Shevaun. She wanted to know that her pain was her own, as was her anger. Even if Adjila could not or would not fix whatever else was wrong with her, at least she would truly be herself.

Adjila nodded and left the kitchen to kneel by Shevaun's side. The vampire was still unconscious, wrapped in a gray-black miasma like smoke.

Erin practically twitched with rising anxiety. She wanted this over with, but at the same time, she started to wonder: Who would she be once Shevaun was gone? Would the things she had learned from her connection to Shevaun—everything from how to fence to how to speak Greek—still be hers, or would all that knowledge just disappear?

Adjila said, "I'm sure one of you has a cell phone."

Sassy handed his over. Erin had discussed with him the merits of calling for help while they had been locked, without food, in the basement, but Sassy had encouraged her to wait. Even then, he had been convinced that Adjila was their best bet for help.

"Alexander, I need to speak to Pandora." Adjila rubbed his temples in frustration. "I know she hates telephones, but I'm needed here and I'm not about to send one of the girls there on her own. . . . Then just tell her I need to see her. She knows where to find me. Tell her . . ." His gaze drifted to Sassy, who frowned in response. "Tell her I've found an interesting potential student, but I need her help to ensure his cooperation." He hung up and shrugged. "She'll show. Erin, come here."

She approached Adjila and Shevaun cautiously, hoping Shevaun would stay as unresponsive as she was at the moment.

"Sassy, stay with Erin. Erin . . ." She didn't like the expression on his face when he looked at her. "Shevaun's mind might be encroaching on yours in a damaging way, but her power is also helping keep your mind contained. When I sever that connection, I don't know exactly what will happen, but I imagine it is going to be deeply unpleasant for you. Keep yourself as calm as you can, and once Shevaun is stabilized, I will come back to try to figure out what to do with you."

She tried not to watch Adjila. Instead, she held on to Sassy. He looked into her eyes, ran a hand down her hair, and kissed her forehead.

The sensation could only be described as one of unraveling.

"It's okay," she heard Sassy saying. "Stay with me, Erin. Erin, can you hear me?" She tried to listen to him instead of the screaming that had started at the base of her brain and was slowly trying to fight its way to her mouth.

No! You won't kill me!

Erin turned at the sound of a shout she knew wasn't there, and found herself inside a memory that both was and wasn't hers.

Shevaun looked down at her hands, which were so small, so frail, the way Erin's had been when she was a child. They were covered in mud from summertime play.

I'm a child again, *Shevaun thought.* My heart beats. My lungs move to breathe even without my willing it.

She stood and wandered. . . .

Erin awoke in the hospital three days later, from what was her first full dissociative episode.

Then Erin was back inside the ruined church, with the same Shevaun who had once looked down at their child's hands with wonder and joy. She was hunched in one of the half-melted pews, weeping.

Erin started to move toward her, drawn by an instinctive desire to soothe her pain, but then she heard a cry from the opposite direction. She turned to find another Shevaun, armed with two long blades, fighting *another* version of herself.

Time to sit down, Erin, she thought.

She tried to remember Adjila's warning, but this didn't make any *sense.* Given what the witch had told her, she had expected that she—Erin—might come apart, that she would struggle to hold herself together. Instead, she stood in the middle of a ruined church that was obviously a product of Shevaun's mind, watching a score of Shevauns weep, laugh, and fight.

The one who remembered being a child held up a hand and stared at it.

"I thought," she said, "that I was being given another chance, at a family, and a future."

"We *have* a family!" another of the Shevauns cried, objecting. "And we're *immortal*. How much more of a future can you want?"

Erin stepped back as those two commenced a yelling argument. She moved toward the church doors, wondering if she could flee this insane projection of . . . *something*. This didn't even seem to be her own madness; it had to be Shevaun's.

Before she reached the door, though, one of the Shevauns grabbed her.

"We won't let you kill us," this one said.

"I'm not trying to kill you!" Erin shouted. "I just want to put you back in your brain and me back in mine." She tried to pull free, but another Shevaun was already reaching for her.

Chapter 23

"WHAT'S GOING ON?" Sassy demanded.

He didn't know who he expected to answer. Erin was staring vacantly into space, unresponsive. Adjila had collapsed. Shevaun was screaming and ranting in what sounded like Latin.

The chaos was enough to make the animal inside him start crying, a keening wail at its captivity and inability to fight back. Part of him wanted to run away, carrying Erin, but though he was certain he could do it, he knew it wouldn't do them any good.

He forced himself to walk toward Adjila, prepared to shake him, hit him, something.

He jumped when the front door of the house opened, and returned protectively to Erin's side as two figures crossed the threshold. The woman had bright, nearly electric blue eyes and umber hair. Behind her walked an abashed-looking man with golden hair and eyes.

The expression on the woman's face was disdainful, to say the least, as she picked up Adjila by one arm; he hung as limp as a puppet in her grip for a moment before she shook her head and dropped him. The man winced as Adjila hit the floor.

"Idiot," she said.

"Pandora?" Sassy inquired, though he was pretty sure he knew the answer.

"Puppy," she responded, with a nod of greeting. The word didn't even sound intentionally demeaning coming from her. He had a sense that everything she said would have that tone. "Alexander, try to do something useful. Wake up the vampire and let her feed. I'll deal with my *other* wayward student."

"What's going on?" Sassy asked.

He didn't expect her to answer him, and was surprised when she didn't dismiss him instantly. Instead, she said, "Two brains, and far too many Shevauns."

"I don't understand."

She waved a hand, a vague gesture that seemed to be a prelude to what she obviously felt was an extreme simplification of the situation. "For the last sixteen years, Erin's mind has been picking up bits and pieces of Shevaun's. Erin holds dozens, maybe hundreds, of variations of Shevaun's history and personality inside her. My fool of a student tried to break the bond without realizing that it would cause a backlash as all those separate forms of Shevaun's personality fought to find a place and a way to preserve their existence."

"Psychotic musical chairs," Sassy said, summarizing. "What about Erin?"

"Her likelihood of finding a seat on her own is slim," Pandora admitted. "It would help if she had more natural power to draw from, to rebuild her mind's defenses from the inside while Adjila pushes from the outside. Now hush so I can wake him up. I dislike Shevaun enough already without her squatting in Adjila's brain like a tumor."

"Wait! Please, can you help Erin?"

This time Pandora didn't respond. She knelt next to Adjila and put one hand over his heart and the other on his forehead, then closed her eyes.

Meanwhile, Alexander was struggling to control Shevaun. He let out a yelp as the vampire managed to latch her fangs on to his wrist, but he didn't push her away, just shut his eyes.

Sassy realized he was biting his own lip only when he tasted blood.

"Erin," he whispered to her still, rigid form. "You've got to come back to me."

He hated feeling helpless. He had been able to talk himself out of almost any trouble he had ever been in. But all the quick scenarios and lies and stories he could come up with at a moment's notice were useless now.

He looked down and realized that his nails were digging into his arms, drawing crescents of blood. He had to change soon, or when he did, it was going to be violent.

"Think, Sassy," he said out loud. *"Think."*

Alexander opened his eyes. His expression was unfocused and his voice tight as he forced out the words "I just wanted to help Erin. Pandora knew about the connection with Shevaun. Kept hiding her from SingleEarth to protect Adjila. I tried to tell one of SingleEarth's people about Erin, so they could help her. She was supposed to call SingleEarth. Not hunters."

Alexander had to be talking about Marissa. She was the only person from SingleEarth close to Erin. She must have panicked when the Triste talked to her.

"Past is past," Sassy managed to say. "Have any *useful* information, right now?"

Alexander nodded sharply. "Erin needs more power."

"Can you *give* her more power?"

"I—" Alexander gasped and turned back to Shevaun, shaking his head. He started murmuring to her and struggled to pry his wrist from her grip.

Sassy looked back at Erin, wondering if what he was thinking made any sense at all or was just a product of the animal yapping inside his mind, telling him to hurry along, get outside, and take his fur. He tried asking Alexander again, but the witch ignored him this time.

It might not even work.

But what if it *did* work?

Erin could heal herself to an extent, if only she had more personal power. If she wasn't human. The tiny amount of shapeshifter blood she had in her system had been enough to keep her alive when Shevaun had hurt her. What would more do?

In the kitchen, he found the tools he needed, including a wicked-looking fillet knife. Sassy didn't fear blades, but for this to work, there would have to be a *lot* of blood involved. If it went wrong, it would go really wrong for both of them.

If this killed him, at least he wouldn't have to worry about meeting Erin's gaze ever again. He bit his lip and then set someone's best knife to his left forearm, pulling the blade in one sweeping motion from his wrist to his elbow. The knife was sharp enough that it didn't even hurt much, but the blood came quickly.

With a string of expletives, he repeated the move on Erin's right arm.

He had to move fast now.

Blood to blood. He grabbed Erin's hand and held on, pressing their forearms together as tightly as possible as he used his other hand and his teeth to wind plastic wrap around and around, keeping the blood in, keeping them connected and, with luck, keeping them from bleeding to death.

Some people chanted "om." Sassy preferred something with one more letter, starting with an *F*. It had a nice ring to it as he whispered it like a mantra under his breath, now fighting dizziness and nausea in addition to the hyena. If he passed out, he wouldn't have to change, right?

Chapter 24

SHEVAUN WHIMPERED. TOO MUCH. It was all too much. The shouting had to stop, only the shouting was coming from her and she didn't know how to stop it.

Please, please just be quiet and let me sleep again.

When she realized she was cradled in Alexander's arms—Alexander, who had once called her a heathen and worse—with his blood in her mouth, Shevaun would have laughed if she could have. But every time she managed to pull air into her lungs, it released itself in a scream.

"You're going to be all right," Alexander said, with barely a hint of a disgusted growl in his voice.

Suddenly, the shouting wasn't just inside her, but also outside, as Brittany and Iana stormed into the room. "What have you *done?*" Brittany shouted while Iana struggled to keep her sister from attacking Pandora.

This is our family, Shevaun tried to tell the voices inside, who were crying things like *life* and *mortal* and *what if?*

"Fine. I'll just take Adjila and go," Pandora said calmly as Brittany continued to shout at her. "It's no skin off my back if you're left with a mad vampire and—"

"*No.*" That was Alexander. "You let this happen. You should—"

"I should *what*?" Pandora replied. "Adjila made this mess, not me."

"He created it, but you knew about it. You could have stopped it when you first discovered it. You could have given the girl her life without ever letting anyone get hurt or putting Adjila or Shevaun in danger. Instead, you let an innocent girl suffer in one of your experiments."

"I don't believe in innocence and you know it," Pandora said, sounding offhand, "and I don't believe in coddling my students. If Adjila couldn't deal with his own problems, he never would have lasted this long."

Out the corner of her eye, Shevaun saw Adjila struggling to get to his feet. If he could do it, she should be able to—

"Don't try to move yet," Alexander advised.

"Come, Alexander. Adjila is fine now. We're leaving."

Alexander hesitated but eventually obeyed his teacher and set Shevaun gently back on the couch as he went to Pandora's side.

Adjila, though, had stood. He appeared unsteady on his feet, but his voice never wavered. "You *will* help," he said, "because you know I would die for her. And if necessary, I will die to avenge her. Are you ready to destroy me?

Because if Alexander is right and you're the one who repeatedly cut off SingleEarth's attempts to contact Erin, so that they couldn't untie this knot before it was ever a problem, *you* are the one I'm going to blame."

Shevaun focused on their conversation, which seemed to be real, and tried to filter out all the other voices and the false images circling the periphery of her vision.

"Idiot student. Idiots, all of you." Pandora sighed. "Fine. I'll help you seal off Shevaun's mind from the other personalities assaulting it. It should heal itself, leaving her at least as sane or stable as she ever was. Then it will be safe for you to do whatever you like with the girl."

Erin, do you know where you are? Do you know who I am?

Where—what have you done to me?

Shevaun felt trapped, like she was locked in a small room with physical restraints—but no, that had never happened, not to *her*. And it wasn't happening now. She was Shevaun. And she could control this. She just had to keep focused.

"What about Erin? Her mind is still damaged," Adjila said. "I need your help to fix it."

Pandora laughed out loud. "Shevaun's mind is mostly contained, if not sound. Erin's has never been a singular, self-sufficient entity. Your puppy has the right idea, but either it will work or it won't. There is nothing more to be done."

"If she dies, he'll be completely intractable," Adjila said.

"Yes, and your mention of a possible student is the only

thing that brought me here. I approve of him, by the way. But he's your student and Erin is your mess and I'm not your mother to nursemaid you."

Another, hoarse voice said, "I'm not . . . liking the student talk." Mm, the puppy. Thinking about him brought another run of images, and the scent of earth and rain. "We live though this and I never want to see you all again."

"There's no reason for you to die now," Pandora said dismissively. "Adjila, make sure he doesn't bleed to death while I fix up your vampire. You two, whatever your names are," she said, glancing back at Iana and Brittany, "I'm going to need power."

"No," Shevaun managed to say, but the girls didn't heed her.

Adjila did. "You know that if you hurt them, Shevaun will break your neck even if it kills her and me both?"

"I'm aware of her attachment to her 'girls.' I won't damage them."

Adjila nodded, and Shevaun had to trust him. Convinced of her family's safety, Shevaun stopped trying to follow the heated conversation between Pandora and the girls and instead focused on Adjila's calming voice.

"I can teach you how to control the change," Adjila was saying to the boy. "And that's the least of it. I can also teach Erin how to control her abilities."

"Don't need your help," Sassy replied. "I can teach her about being a shifter. If this works."

"It's not that simple. The damage to her mind and her

longtime connection to Shevaun is going to have lingering effects you won't be able to tackle on your own," Adjila said, his tone still soft and even. "Her hallucinations indicate an ability to see power auras, and perhaps hear thoughts. Psychic ability like that, without training, can drive even a healthy human being mad. I think we agree that Erin does not need additional strain. How much more you decide to study . . . that's up to you."

The promise would be enough to keep the boy from trying to disappear the instant this was over. Shevaun didn't want him to disappear. He and Erin reminded her of herself and Adjila, when they had both been young and learning the rules of their new world—and learning how to break them.

Shevaun's attention was pulled away from Adjila and Sassy as Pandora gripped her wrist hard enough to grind the bones together. Her eyes flew open, and she tried to focus them so that she could object.

"Good, you're still in there," Pandora whispered. "This is going to hurt."

Chapter 25

ERIN WATCHED AS VARIOUS VERSIONS of Shevaun killed each other around her in the melting church.

Only one, who had been a child with Erin, had taken up a post defending Erin. Or guarding her; Erin wasn't sure. This Shevaun was motherly in a bloody fashion, and alternated between expressing a desire to protect Erin for her own sake and a concern that if Erin was killed, this whole place would disintegrate before anyone else could control it.

They had been challenged only a handful of times, and Erin's self-appointed guardian had made quick work of those who tried. The others were all occupied with each other. When one of them lost, that particular Shevaun faded, melting into the remnants of the church. Some lingered in the forms of portraits or idols, like wax figures standing eerily in the chaotic mindscape, but some left nothing but a stain or a shadow.

"This is sick," Erin said.

"Most of them couldn't survive independently anyway," her guardian said. "Even if they could win this fight, most of them are nothing but two-dimensional constructs, housing some single key memory or impulse. They are nothing but Shevaun's desire to fight and hunt, born of your years in captivity."

"What about you?" When this was all over, would the woman who was currently protecting her decide to take control of this fractured world?

"I'm the oldest," the woman said. "I've been with you the longest. We grew up together. That means I am the most complete."

"Shouldn't you be in *Shevaun's* brain, then? Not mine?"

The woman smiled sadly. "The most complete, except for *her.* Many of us are fighting over there, too, but if anyone but the original takes control of Shevaun's body, Adjila will destroy it. Most of them don't realize that, or don't believe it."

"Why would he kill you?" Erin asked. "He loves you."

"He loves *Shevaun.* I am not her. I have many of her memories, but I have grown up with you. There isn't one of us who could pass for her for any length of time, and many of us wouldn't even try. The witch who created us is fully capable of destroying the consequences of his own actions. He—" She stopped as the ground shook under their feet, and ancient trees began to emerge from the ground. The night sky was visible through the last shards of the once domed ceiling. "Time to end this. Stay here."

Erin did as commanded, because she didn't have a choice. There was nowhere else she could go as the eldest of her alters faced off with the half dozen Shevauns still fighting. She broke one's neck but barely had to touch the rest. She pressed a hand to one's forehead; that Shevaun collapsed like a doll. Another tried to grab her, but when the older one's hands touched the younger one, the two women became one.

Around them, as they fought, the church rebuilt itself. It looked different now. The walls were panels of stained glass set between the trunks of ancient trees. The dome above was a canopy of intertwined leaves painted with elaborate murals.

Once she had disposed of the other alters, the remaining Shevaun—the *last* Shevaun—walked back to Erin.

"My turn now?" Erin asked, trying to brace herself. Would she still be aware but unable to interact with anything? Or would she just fade out of existence and into nothingness like the others had?

But there was something in the way the auburn-haired woman was looking at her.

"I told you, I grew up with you. I could never kill you," the woman said. Then she smiled and tossed her head. "Even without *that* guarding you."

"That?" Erin repeated, and turned to find a vaguely familiar canine, with low shoulders and oversized round ears, behind her. Its fur was creamy gold, with brown-black spots, and it tilted its head curiously as she approached it.

Overhead the leafy canopy broke just enough to reveal the moon.

The animal threw back its head and let out a yipping, chortling cry. It should have been frightening, but it made Erin laugh. She heard Shevaun chuckle, but when she turned, she caught only the shadow of the other woman slipping between the trees and out of the clearing.

Erin? Erin, can you hear me?

She didn't know where the voice was coming from. She looked around, trying to locate it. *"Sassy?"* she called.

Adjila says the hyena should be able to lead you out of your mind and back into your skin.

"Hyena?"

Yeah. They're not real big on philosophy and introspection. Give it control, and it will find its way back into the real world.

Give it control. Was he implying that she was exercising any control at all at the moment? The hyena was running around in hyperactive circles, darting in and out of the trees and, on occasion, pausing to chase its own tail.

Well. Worth a shot.

Erin sat down and closed her eyes.

She returned to the real world just in time to hear the front door slam as someone walked out. As she struggled to open her eyes, she discovered that she was wrapped in Sassy's arms, her head buried against his chest.

Adjila knelt near them, looking too exhausted even to stand. He tried to but ended up falling and half crawled to the couch, where Shevaun lay with Brittany and Iana. The three of them were conscious but looked too tired even to lift their heads.

Erin sat up and ran her hands along her arms, which were so itchy she felt like there were ants crawling beneath her skin. Sassy grabbed on to her as she stood; he twined his fingers with hers and caught her gaze, stopping her from scratching at the phantom sensation.

He glanced back at Adjila and the others just long enough to ask, "Will all of you be okay?"

"We'll rest, and then hunt. Best to be gone before then," Adjila advised. "Come back after dawn. I imagine you'll want that long to run anyway."

Sassy nodded.

"I don't understand," Erin said as she followed him out the back door.

But the instant she was standing at the edge of the woods behind the house, bathed in the moon's light, she felt like she understood *everything*.

"Come on, my crazy girl," Sassy said, tugging her hand as they hurried into the woods. "Let me show you how it's done."

Then things got funny again. She recalled mixed-up images of the forest, of running and jumping, but it wasn't scary or alien the way the church had been. At last she opened her eyes once more, with a very familiar feeling of *I've lost time.*

"Erin!"

Sassy flung himself at her, knocking her backward. They were still outside, but it was dawn, and they both had dirt on their skin and clothes.

"Morning," he said, a little more subdued.

"Where—"

"Woods behind the house where Adjila and Shevaun have been staying," Sassy answered, his words practically running together as he spoke. "It's Saturday. The first couple of changes kind of fry your memory, but I kept you out of trouble. How is . . . How are you? I knew you wouldn't be in any shape to talk when you first woke up, at least until the moon was down. I—" The first rush of energy had left him, and now he seemed uncertain again. "I had to decide, so I made you what I am. It's what kept you alive, but it's probably going to take some getting used to. Some of the shifters have it good, but my . . . our . . . kind has it kind of rough, especially at first. I'll help you though, unless you want me out of your life. I know you didn't choose this."

Let the puppy stay. Erin jumped at the voice, which seemed to be coming from right beside her. But no one was there—not outside, at least. *He saved our life.*

"Erin?" Sassy asked.

"One of the Shevauns stuck around," she replied. *Are*

you . . . there? she thought. She had never been able to hear her alter before.

I'm here. And I'm staying, but you can hold the reins unless you need me, Shevaun answered. *But keep the puppy. He's good to us.*

"Of course I'm keeping the puppy," Erin replied. She clapped a hand over her mouth as she realized she had spoken out loud, but Sassy just laughed. "Why do I feel even crazier today than I did yesterday?"

"Because real life is stranger than any delusion you could come up with," Sassy said seriously. "And usually scarier than any hospital."

"I *could* still be hallucinating," Erin pointed out, knowing full well that nothing here felt like a hallucination. She could smell the earth around her, and the trees. And if she wasn't mistaken, she could smell bacon cooking somewhere.

"Is it a nice hallucination?" Sassy asked.

She linked an arm with his. It felt natural, and it made him smile, erasing the last of the nervousness from his face. "Yeah, I guess it's okay."

Such a way with words, Shevaun said dryly.

To which the hyena added suavely, *Bacon!*

"Adjila asked us to come back after dawn," he said. "There's talk about teaching me, and maybe you, too, how to use power. Maybe how to be the kind of awesome immortal witch he is."

"I don't need to be awesome or immortal," Erin said. "I'm just happy to be *me*."

Epilogue

THE OPEN SKY still made Erin nervous. It probably would for a long time. Having no boundaries but her own skin and bones between her and the twenty-two acres of forest that Adjila and Shevaun had given them permission to use made Erin feel as if she could unravel like Ariadne's thread in the labyrinth.

She lay on a litter of pine needles, watching the sky through a break in the trees above. The full moon—the *hunter's* moon—hung heavy and white, and marked one year since the events that had so drastically altered her life.

In her other world, there was homework to do. She had agreed to help Marissa study for her French midterm, and Erin needed to study for her own exams; after all, she had to keep her grades up to stay eligible for the fencing team. And of course there were SATs to take if she ever planned to apply to college—which she did.

There was still so much to learn about herself. SingleEarth had told her father some long-winded story to explain her recovery and complete independence from medication, but Erin hoped to tell him the truth someday.

That was her other life, though. In this world, she lay on the loam and felt the moonlight on her skin, letting it push her until all the voices inside were shouting, *We want to run!*

Sharp, laughter-like barking brought her to her paws. She stretched and then returned Sassy's greeting with a yip of her own.

She opened all the aspects of her self to the forest: Erin, who still feared her freedom but trusted Sassy and was slowly beginning to trust herself; the hyena, who simply wanted to play, with no concern for the "real" world beyond the forest's edge; and Shevaun, whose voice was softer every day, until sometimes it was hard to distinguish what was left of her from Erin.

All three minds were in agreement: *Time to hunt. Time to run.*

ABOUT THE AUTHOR

Amelia Atwater-Rhodes grew up in Concord, Massachusetts. Born in 1984, she wrote her first novel, *In the Forests of the Night,* praised as "remarkable" (*Voice of Youth Advocates*) and "mature and polished" (*Booklist*), when she was thirteen. Other books in the Den of Shadows series are *Demon in My View, Shattered Mirror,* and *Midnight Predator,* all ALA-YALSA Quick Picks. She has also published the five-volume series The Kiesha'ra: *Hawksong,* a *School Library Journal* Best Book of the Year and a *Voice of Youth Advocates* Best Science Fiction, Fantasy, and Horror Selection; *Snakecharm; Falcondance; Wolfcry,* an IRA-CBC Young Adults' Choice; and *Wyvernhail.*